W9-AWY-095

THIS BOOK
BELONGS TO

- - - - - - - - - - - - - - -

- - - - - - - - - - - - -

SELBY
SPEAKS

SELBY
SPEAKS

DUNCAN BALL

with illustrations by Allan Stomann

Angus&Robertson
An imprint of HarperCollins*Publishers*

Angus&Robertson
An imprint of HarperCollins*Publishers*, Australia

First published in Australia in 1988
This edition published in 2005
by HarperCollins*Publishers* Pty Limited
ABN 36 009 913 517
A member of the HarperCollins*Publishers* (Australia) Pty Limited Group
www.harpercollins.com.au

HarperCollins*Publishers*
25 Ryde Road, Pymble, Sydney, NSW 2073, Australia
31 View Road, Glenfield, Auckland 10, New Zealand
77–85 Fulham Palace Road, London W6 8JB, United Kingdom
2 Bloor Street East, 20th floor, Toronto, Ontario M4W 1A8, Canada
10 East 53rd Street, New York NY 10022, USA

National Library of Australia Cataloguing-in-Publication data:

Ball, Duncan, 1941– .
  Selby speaks.
  ISBN 0 2072 0024 6.
  1. Dogs – Juvenile fiction. I. Stomann, Allan. II. Title.
A823'.3

Cover and internal design by Christabella Designs
Typeset in 14/18 Bembo by Helen Beard, ECJ Australia Pty Limited
Printed and bound in Australia by Griffin Press on 60gsm Bulky Paperback

6 5 4 3   06 07 08

For Ian, who knows Selby
as well as anyone

CONTENTS

BEFOREWORD

These stories are partly about those lovely lovely wonderful people, the Trifles-my favourite people in the whole world. But mostly, they're about me and the crazy things that can happen to a talking dog. I'm in every one of them and they're ~~mostly~~ absolutely true.

As I write this note, I'm hiding under the dining room table and Dr and Mrs Trifle are in front of the T.V., snoring away. I'd better stop now before they wake up and catch me writing.

Just remember: this is no ordinary book. When you touch this you touch a dog. (Me.)

Selby

xi

PINK PANIC

Selby was the only talking dog in Australia. For all he knew he was the only talking dog in the whole world. He was born an ordinary dog but had learned to talk while watching TV with his owners, Dr and Mrs Trifle, in their home in the little town of Bogusville.

It all began one day when Selby realised that he could understand everything that was being said on TV. Learning to talk was another matter. Selby spent hours and hours when the Trifles were out of the house repeating what the people on television were saying until, finally, he could speak perfectly. But before the thrill of learning to talk had worn off, Selby panicked. What would happen when people discovered that he could talk? At first the Trifles would be happy to have a talking dog for a pet, but soon they'd ask him to do things around the house. They'd have him answering the telephone or mowing the lawn or even going out to the shops.

"I don't want to be their servant," Selby thought. "I want to be their pet."

It could even be worse: the Trifles might send him off to a laboratory where he would spend the rest of his life answering scientists' stupid questions. And that would never do.

"I like my life just the way it is," he thought, "and I'm going to keep my talking a secret even if it kills me!"

Selby almost gave away his secret many times. One of the closest calls was the day he was swinging on branches and vines through the jungle when suddenly a branch broke and he fell and was grabbed by cannibals and thrown into a pot. But just as he splashed into the lukewarm water he woke up screaming, "No! No! Don't cook me! I'm Selby, the only talking dog in the world!" It was only when he looked around him and saw that he was lying safely on a carpet in the Trifles' house in Bogusville that he realised he'd been having a bad dream.

"I probably ate too many of those awful Dry-Mouth Dog Biscuits Mrs Trifle keeps feeding me. They always upset my stomach and give me nightmares," Selby thought as he dashed to the front window, opened it, and saw that the car was gone. "Thank goodness the Trifles have gone out. I'm just lucky they didn't hear me talking."

In fact the only one who *had* heard Selby talk was Pinky, a pet galah which the Trifles were minding for Mrs Trifle's cousin Wilhemina.

Selby put his paws up on the tall cage and stared at the little bird.

"Hello Pinks. Say something to me. Say, 'Hello, Selby my good friend,'" Selby said, knowing full well that the only thing Pinky ever said was, "*Help! I'm drowning!*" — exactly what Cousin Wil had screamed when she fell in a fish pond during a garden party ten years before. "'*Help! I'm drowning!*' is a strange thing for a galah to say," Selby added. "I suspect Cousin Wil screamed so loud that it got stuck in your little pea-brain. Go ahead, my little panic merchant, say it. Say, '*Help! I'm drowning!*'"

"I'm Selby," Pinky screeched, "the only talking dog in the world!"

Selby froze like a statue.

"What did you say?" he asked.

"I'm Selby, the only talking dog in the world!" Pinky squawked again.

"That's what I thought you said," Selby said. "Now, you aren't Selby, I am. So shut your beak before you give away my secret and ruin my life forever."

"I'm Selby," Pinky screeched even louder, "the only talking dog in the world! *Squawk.*"

"You're supposed to say, '*Help! I'm drowning!*'" Selby yelled as he wondered how long it would be till the Trifles returned.

"I'm Selby, *squawk*, the only talking dog in the world!"

"I've got it," Selby thought as he put his face up to the cage. "Maybe if I scream really loud he'll repeat what I say. *Help! I'm drowning!*" Selby cried at the top of his lungs.

Pinky's eyes popped open at the sight of the screaming dog. In a fright he flew against the side of the cage, knocking it to the ground. All of which would have been okay if the cage hadn't broken in two. In a second Pinky was free and flying around the room.

"Come back here you silly seed-swallower!" Selby yelled, chasing him. "You're not supposed to be flying around loose!"

"I'm Selby, the only talking dog in the world!" Pinky squawked and, before Selby could head him off, Pinky had disappeared out the window and into the cold night air.

"Come back here you little twittering tattle-tale!" Selby yelled. "You can't survive out there! It's too cold. And besides, you don't know how to find food! You've been in a cage all your life! Why am I wasting my breath talking to a bird?" he asked himself.

Selby stared out into the darkness for a glimpse of Pinky.

"This is terrible," Selby said, feeling suddenly sad. "The Trifles will be awfully upset when they come home and find Pinky gone. Of course, they won't know it's all my fault. They'll think Pinky knocked his cage over and broke it — which is true. And they'll think *they* left the window open — because they're kind of absent-minded about those things. Pinky will fly away and freeze or starve to death. This is awful," Selby said, blinking back a tear. "But I guess he won't be blabbing out my secret."

Then, from the top branches of the silky oak in the front yard, came a terrible cry which pierced the night air:

"*I'm Selby*, squawk, *the only talking dog in the world!*"

"All right, big mouth!" Selby yelled as he jumped out the window and looked up at Pinky. "Shut up or everyone in Bogusville will hear you!"

Suddenly Selby remembered his swinging-through-the-jungle-on-branches-and-vines dream.

"My only chance is to get to the top of that tree," he thought. "I'll grab little Pinky and scream 'Help! I'm drowning!' in his face so loud that he has to repeat it."

Limb by limb Selby crept up the tree towards the unsuspecting parrot. In a minute he was hidden in a clump of leaves on the top branch, only a leg's length from Pinky.

"I'll make a sudden lunge," Selby thought, "and grab him. He won't know what hit him."

Selby sprang forward and grabbed the stunned Pinky with his front paws, teetering for a second on the thin branch. Then, just when Selby had screamed out the Help! part of Help! I'm drowning! there was a crack and a thwack and a twang and Selby and Pinky hurtled down through the leaves toward the ground.

"I'm falling!" Selby screamed, and before he knew it he was staggering around the front lawn. After a moment of staggering in circles, Selby fell into a bush, unconscious.

He woke a few minutes later to the sound of running feet and Mrs Trifle's voice.

"He's dead! He's dead!" she yelled as she dashed down the path and picked Pinky up, not noticing Selby in the bushes. "Oh, Pinkums, how will I ever explain this to Cousin Wil?"

"I don't think he's dead," Dr Trifle said. "He's just unconscious. Look he's opening his eyes. He's moving his beak. I think he's about to say something."

"Oh, no!" Selby thought, feeling suddenly happy about Pinky being alive and then

instantly sad. "In a minute the news will be out. I'm done. I might as well confess. It's better they should hear it from the dog's mouth than from that big-beaked blabbermouth."

Selby stepped out of the bushes and was about to say, "I confess. I can talk. I don't care who knows it now. Go ahead and send me off to a laboratory to be asked stupid questions by scientists for the rest of my life," when Pinky screeched:

"Help! I'm falling!"

"'Help? I'm falling?'" Mrs Trifle asked. "Did he say falling? That's very odd."

"I do believe he did," Dr Trifle said thoughtfully. "Well, at least it's a lot better than 'Help! I'm drowning!'"

"And it's even better than," Selby thought as he shook himself off and started on his evening walk, "some of the other things he's been saying lately."

SELBY GETS DR TRIFLE'S GOTE

"You've bought a goat?" Mrs Trifle said to Dr Trifle as she finished putting the washing in the clothes basket.

"I didn't buy it, I *made* it," said Dr Trifle, who spent most of his time inventing things. "And it's not really a goat. It's a GOTE."

"I see," said Mrs Trifle, who didn't really.

"I mean GOTE, spelled G-O-T-E," Dr Trifle said.

Selby watched from deep within the bushes where he lay secretly reading through his collection of *Wonderful Wanda* comic strips as

10

Dr Trifle carried his latest invention into the backyard and put it down on the lawn.

"GOTE stands for Gyrating Oscillating Transistorised Emulsifier," Dr Trifle explained.

"And what exactly does a Gyrating Oscillating Transistorised Emulsifier do?" asked Mrs Trifle, who was the mayor of Bogusville and knew a lot of big words but not those particular ones.

"Just what the name says," Dr Trifle said. "It takes bits of certain herbaceous matter and masticates them into an emulsion."

"It whats?"

"I suppose you might call it . . . well, sort of a lawn-mower."

"A lawn-mower?" Mrs Trifle asked.

"Or should I say, a *lawn-muncher*?" Dr Trifle said. "I've named this one Howard. Turn Howard on and he runs around munching away till you turn him off again. Howard is going to revolutionise grass cutting as we know it."

"What exactly," Mrs Trifle asked, "is wrong with grass cutting as we know it?"

"Too noisy," Dr Trifle said. "And too monotonous. I get so bored pushing that silly lawn-mower around in circles. Howard, here, will roam around, quietly munching and crunching, like those things that run around swimming pools eating up all the muck. Besides, a properly munched lawn looks much better than a cut lawn."

"It does?" Mrs Trifle asked.

"Well, of course it does," Dr Trifle, who wasn't quite sure why it did, explained. "Here. Watch this."

Dr Trifle poured a few drops of petrol in Howard's left ear, and turned the GOTE around, pointing it towards a patch of long grass.

"That tiny bit of petrol is enough to keep Howard running for exactly five minutes. Now for the magic words: *munchum crunchum diddlie dunchum*," Dr Trifle said and Howard's red eyes lit up as he grabbed a mouthful of grass and started to chew.

"That's amazing!" Mrs Trifle said, nearly dropping her clean laundry. "How did you do that?"

"Howard is voice-activated," Dr Trifle explained. "Say the right words and off he goes."

"But why *munchum crunchum*?" asked Mrs Trifle. "Why not tell him something simple like *mow the lawn* and you could add a *please* just to be polite?"

"That would be fine if we lived way off by ourselves. But we don't, you see. We live in Bogusville where there are lots of houses all pushed in together," said Dr Trifle, who loved to explain things. "Now, let's pretend that all our neighbours dash out and buy one of my new GOTEs. And let's pretend that all of them start when someone says, *mow the lawn* — adding a *please* to be polite. What would happen?"

"Well, I'm not sure," said Mrs Trifle, who had begun hanging out the laundry.

"I'll tell you what would happen: there would be pandemonium!" Dr Trifle said, waving his arms around.

"Panda what?" Mrs Trifle asked.

"Total confusion," Dr Trifle said. "Someone would yell '*Mow the lawn*' out the window — adding a '*please*' to be polite — and all the GOTEs in the neighbourhood would start munching their way around the lawns, whether they needed munching or not."

"So you're going to give all your GOTEs different code words, so they won't all start up at once," said Mrs Trifle, who was every bit as smart as Dr Trifle.

"Precisely! Words we don't use very often like *munchum crunchum diddlie dunchum* so there won't be any accidental turnings-on."

"We certainly don't say that very often," Mrs Trifle said.

Suddenly Howard stopped and stared down at a weed.

"Watch this," Dr Trifle said. "This is something no ordinary lawn-mower can do."

"Undesirable. Undesirable," the GOTE said in a raspy robot-like voice as he pulled up a weed with his teeth and then carried it to Dr Trifle's Automatic Weed Shredder and dropped it in. As soon as the weed fell, the shredder turned on automatically with a whirr and a grind and the weed was shredded into tiny pieces.

"Thank you, Howard," the Automatic Weed Shredder said to the robot, as Mrs Trifle looked on in amazement.

"Howard is designed to pull up weeds and throw them in the shredder," Dr Trifle said.

"And the shredder even said, 'Thank you,'" Mrs Trifle said as Howard started munching grass again. "Your inventions always have such good manners, dear."

"It doesn't cost any more to be polite. Anyway, you see how the GOTE and the shredder work together. They'll need some minor adjustments but new inventions always need a few minor adjustments. Oh, my goodness," Dr Trifle said suddenly, looking at his watch. "I'd better turn Howard off or we'll be late for your council dinner. We wouldn't want the mayor to be late, would we now?"

"Just let me finish hanging out these clothes before we go," Mrs Trifle added, "so they'll be dry by tomorrow."

"*Stop chop diddlie bop!*" Dr Trifle commanded and Howard went suddenly stiff.

With the Trifles safely out of the house, Selby crept out of the bushes and had a better look at the GOTE.

"That Dr Trifle surely is a clever man," Selby said, peering in Howard's nose to check his oil level. "Everyone in the world will want to own a lawn-muncher like this. You were doing a great job, Howard. Go ahead, now, give us a demonstration. What were those words again? *Munchum crunchum diddlie dunchum?*"

Howard's eyes flickered to life and he started munching his way through a clump of grass. But before he'd finished one mouthful he raised his head, looked over at the clothes that were drying on the clothes line and said, "Undesirable. Undesirable," in a mechanical voice.

"Hey! Stop!" Selby said as he followed the GOTE towards the clothes. "Uh-oh, if I don't stop him he'll tear them off the line and throw them in the weed shredder! I've got to do something fast!"

"*Stop mop diddlie bop*! Or was it, *Stop rop diddlie hop*!" Selby yelled as he grabbed Howard by his short metal tail and was pulled along toward the wet clothes.

"*Stop pop diddlie lop*!" he shrieked, as he tried to tip the GOTE over. "I'm ordering you to stop!"

Selby ran ahead grabbing the clothes from the clothes line but soon Howard was there, reaching for a pair of dangling underpants.

"Undesirable. Undesirable," the GOTE said.

"Get away from those!" Selby screamed, snatching the undies, three shirts, seventeen socks and a towel just as Howard was about to grab them.

"Undesirable," Howard said again as he snapped at a purple sock just as Selby rescued it.

"I can't stand it," Selby said, now weighed down by a huge load of laundry. "I can't keep ahead of this beast! Oh, no! He's going for Mrs Trifle's favourite floral frock!"

Selby turned to snatch the frock and felt something strange clutch his tail.

"Something strange is clutching my tail," Selby thought. "I wonder what it could be?" he added as he grabbed the last bit of laundry. "It feels kind of like some sort of metal mouth with metal teeth. I wonder ... *Yooooooooooouwwwwwch*!" Selby screeched, dropping the clothes as Howard's mouth clamped shut and the GOTE began dragging Selby across the lawn. "Let go of me, you grass-munching moron!"

"Undesirable," Howard muttered mechanically with a mouth full of dog. "Undesirable."

"Let go of me! I'm not a weed! I can prove it!" Selby screamed. "Hey! Where are you taking me? Not to the Automatic Weed Shredder? No, please! Howard, be reasonable! Can't we talk this over?!"

"Undesirable," Howard said as he lifted the struggling Selby over the shredder.

"I'm gone!" Selby screamed as he fell towards the blades of the machine, expecting them to whirr into action. But instead the shredder shook, lurched — made a noise that

sounded something like a mechanical burp —
and then spat him out onto the ground.

"You're right, Howard," the shredder said
slowly. "Undesirable."

The bewildered Selby looked up just in time
to see Howard slowly come to a stop as he ran
out of petrol. Blinking his red eyes, the GOTE
said, "Undesirabllllllllllll," and then was silent.

"As for those minor adjustments Dr Trifle
was talking about, Howard," Selby muttered as
he dashed around picking up clothes and
hanging them back on the clothes line. "If you
and that silly shredder can't tell the difference
between an undesirable weed and yours truly,
the most desirable dog in the world, then you're
going to need more than just minor
adjustments."

THE INCREDIBLE SHRINKING DOG

"Help! I'm shrinking!" Selby thought. "I'm getting littler by the minute!"

It had all started the night before when Selby went to the Bogusville Bijou Theatre to see a film called *The Incredible Shrinking Teenager*.

"It's my birthday tomorrow," he thought as he snaked past the queue and hid behind a seat till the lights went out, "and I'm going to see a movie as a special birthday treat. I might as well

20

give myself a present in case Dr and Mrs Trifle forget. Oh, boy!" Selby thought as he munched a mouthful of popcorn he found on the seat beside him. "I can't wait to see the teenager start shrinking!"

The film was about a boy who ate too much junk food and suddenly began shrinking and shrinking until he was so small that the cat mistook him for a mouse and chased him. All through the film the teenager got smaller until he was so little that he climbed through a keyhole to escape from a hungry spider.

"What a great film!" Selby thought and he felt his heart beating against his tight collar. "I wonder how he's going to get big again?"

Selby munched three chocolate bars that he'd been saving and then sucked a lolly as he watched the Incredible Shrinking Teenager grow big again by forcing himself to eat fresh vegetables.

When it was over, Selby ran home and curled up on the little round cushion he used for a bed — a cushion so small that one of his legs always dangled on the floor. In his sleep he had a terrible nightmare about being so small that an ant chased him round and round the kitchen floor mistaking him for a bit of left-over sausage.

"No! No!" Selby screamed in his dream. "Leave me alone, you six-legged savage! I'm not a sausage. I'm only a medium-sized talking dog!"

Selby woke up suddenly and sprang to his feet, looking around in the darkness for the giant ant.

"I must have been dreaming," he thought as he turned around three times (as he always did before getting settled) and lay down only to notice that his leg didn't dangle out onto the floor the way it usually did. And, what was worse, his collar, which had always been too tight, was suddenly loose!

Selby trotted to the kitchen as his brain began to wake up. He was just about to get a Dry-Mouth Dog Biscuit from his bowl when he noticed that the bowl had grown big in the night!

"Help!" Selby thought as the inescapable and terrifying thought shot through his brain. "I'm shrinking! I'm getting littler by the minute! I'm the Incredible Shrinking Dog! It's just like in the movie! I'm being punished for eating a few chocolate bars and some popcorn. It's not fair! I don't deserve to shrink!" he added, staring angrily at an ant that crawled across his bowl.

Selby ran around the kitchen, opening cupboards and searching through the fridge.

"I've got to have fresh vegies quick before I shrink any more!" he thought. "But the Trifles haven't done the weekly shopping! Where am I going to find vegies at this time of night? Except (*gulp*), except ... from Dr Trifle's vegetable garden."

Selby tore out of the house, yanked up a carrot and gobbled it without even bothering to clean off the dirt. Then he ate two radishes and, before his mouth even had a chance to cool down, he ate three zucchinis, a small lettuce and a couple of onions.

"It worked for the Incredible Shrinking Teenager," Selby said, feeling his stomach filling up and remembering how much he hated vegetables. "I only hope it works for me."

Selby ran along a row of tomatoes, snatching them right and left in his teeth, and then down

a row of rhubarb, leaving behind nothing but a carpet of green leaves. In another minute he'd eaten five cucumbers and a cabbage and was staring greedily at a pumpkin.

"Suddenly I don't feel so well," Selby said, clutching his swollen stomach. "I've never eaten this much of anything in my life — not even when I gobbled the whole chocolate-cream layer cake with hundreds and thousands that Mrs Trifle made on my birthday last year."

Selby staggered back into the house and lay down again on the cushion that was still too big and drifted off to sleep only to be wakened by singing voices coming closer and closer.

"Happy birthday to you," Dr and Mrs Trifle sang. "Happy birthday to you. Happy birthday, dear Selby. Happy birthday to you."

Selby opened his eyes and there were Dr and Mrs Trifle bending over him.

"Poor Selby," Mrs Trifle said, patting him on the head. "I don't suppose he knows it's his birthday. I'm sure he doesn't realise that we finally gave him a bigger sleeping cushion, one that fits him properly."

"And a nice big bowl that fits lots of those lovely Dry-Mouth Dog Biscuits that he likes so much," Dr Trifle added.

"Oh, well," Mrs Trifle said, looking at the new collar she'd put on him when he was sleeping, "here's something he always loves: a chocolate-cream layer cake with hundreds and thousands!"

"Yikes!" thought Selby as he put a paw to his mouth to keep from gagging.

"My goodness!" Dr Trifle said. "Did you see that? One look at that cake and he's gone all green in the face. I do think he's sick of sweets. Maybe we'd better give him a bowl full of fresh vegetables for a change. I'm sure he'd like that."

"What a good idea," Mrs Trifle said. "I'll go and pick some right now. I hope that possum hasn't got into the garden again."

TERRIBLE TINA, TWO-TOOTH TIGER

Selby was just dozing off when Mrs Trifle's dreadful sister, Aunt Jetty, burst into the house having just returned from a tiger hunt in darkest Scotland.

"Darkest Scotland?" Mrs Trifle asked politely, spreading more marmalade on her toast. "You mean to say you were hunting a person eating tiger in Scotland?"

"Not a *person eater*," Aunt Jetty said, thumping her walking-stick on the floor but hitting Selby's tail by mistake. "Tina is quite specifically a *man eater*. She hates men. Or, putting it differently, she

27

loves them — for dinner. Tina was first captured in India many years ago when she terrorised villages and attacked only the men. She never ate a *whole* man, though, because of a shortage in the tooth department —"

"A shortage in the tooth department?" Dr Trifle said, looking up from the plans he was making for a talking floral clock for the Bogusville Memorial Rose Garden.

"A severe shortage. She only has two teeth: an upper and a lower. With only two teeth she couldn't actually kill anyone but you can be sure there are a goodly number of blokes in India with shortages in the finger and toe departments."

"I see," Dr Trifle said, doing a quick count of his fingers and wondering when he'd last cut his fingernails.

"When they finally caught her," Aunt Jetty went on, "they sent her to the Haggis Highland Zoo in Scotland. She loved it there for a while but finally escaped one night and attacked a piper who was playing *Scotland the Brave* on his bagpipes. When they found him the next day his dress was badly torn."

"Kilt," interrupted Mrs Trifle.

"No, he was very much alive," Aunt Jetty continued. "When Tina finally noticed his dress she thought he was a woman, so she left him alone. Anyway, the locals, knowing my reputation as a big game hunter," Aunt Jetty said, polishing her fingernails on her safari jacket, "called me in. All I had to do was to throw a net over the old girl," Aunt Jetty said, throwing her net over Selby and yanking him upside down in the air, "like that! It was dead easy."

"Easy, schmeasy," Selby thought, struggling to stand up in the net but with his feet poking out everywhere. "If she doesn't watch her step she'll meet the world's first woman-eating dog."

Aunt Jetty dumped Selby onto the carpet and watched him jump through the front window and tear away down Bunya-Bunya Crescent.

"I brought old Tina back here when I caught her," she said. "It's finders keepers I reckon. I've just put her in the Bogusville Zoo. She should be happy there."

Selby went for a walk through Bogusville Reserve till dark and then took his usual short cut back through the zoo, squeezing between the bars of the closed front gate.

"There's nothing more peaceful than a zoo at night, when there are no crowds and the animals can relax," Selby said as he made the rounds of the cages, looking at each of his animal friends.

He stopped for a minute and sang a bit from his favourite opera, *Cleopatra and the Asp*, to Bazza the opera-loving boa constrictor and watched as tears of joy formed in the old snake's eyes. And then he poked a handful of hay to Terrence Tusk, the one-tusked elephant.

"How are they treating you, Terry?" Selby asked, not expecting an answer because he, Selby, was the only talking animal in Australia and, for all he knew, the world. "How's the tusk?"

Selby was about to take his usual short cut through the empty cage next to Terrence's when he saw a newly painted sign at the front of it which said:

"Hmmmmmmmm," Selby said, looking closely at the sign. "How am I going to take my short cut? The cage isn't empty any more. They've put an animal in it. But what's an *an eater*? Is it an animal I've never heard of before, some woolly beast that eats *ans*? If so, what's an *an*? Oh, silly me, I know! They must be getting an *anteater* and Postie hasn't painted the T in yet," Selby said, referring to Postie Paterson, Bogusville's postman and part-time helper at the zoo. "Well, anteaters are pretty harmless — at least to dogs. I think I'll take my usual short cut anyway. It's a lot quicker than going all the way back through the front gate."

Selby barged in through the bars of the cage, little knowing that Postie (a not-very-experienced sign-writer who always painted signs backwards because when he painted them frontwards he always ran off the end of the sign) had written a warning sign to say that Two-Tooth Tina was a MAN EATER. He'd started by painting the R and then the E and so on but he hadn't got a chance to paint in the M and finish the sign when closing

31

time came so the sign still only said AN EATER.

As Selby walked through the cage towards the bars at the back he felt a pair of eyes following him in the darkness.

"Hmmmmmmm," he thought. "There's something creepy about this place. I feel like there are eyes following me around in the darkness. It must be that new anteater. I wonder where he is?"

Suddenly there was a great roar and Tina jumped out into the moonlight.

"Yoooooooooowww!" screamed Selby as he backed into a corner. "You're no flippin' anteater! Get away from me! Help!"

Tina roared again and snapped at Selby's front paws. Selby quickly stood on his hind legs and put his front legs over his head.

"It's Tina! What is she doing here? I thought she was still in darkest Scotland! Oh no! Aunt Jetty must have brought her back! Heeeeeeeeelllllllllllp!"

"Roooaaarrr! Arrrrrr!" Tina snarled and her two teeth clicked so fast as she lunged for Selby's feet that it sounded like a high-speed knitting contest.

Selby jumped in the air as she snapped and snapped until he found himself dancing from foot to foot with his front legs still over his head. Then suddenly Tina sat back on her haunches and watched.

"What *is* she doing?" Selby thought, still jumping furiously from foot to foot. "I know! She thinks I'm a Scottish dancer doing a highland fling."

Selby grapped a piece of cardboard from the ground without missing a step and held it to his waist with one paw to make it look like a kilt as homesick tears formed in Tina's big round eyes.

"The Campbells are coming..." Selby sang and his feet hammered the ground in a frenzied blur. "And I've got to be going because I can't (*puff*) keep this up much longer. Heaven's above, how am I going (*puff*) to get out of here with all my toes?"

Just then something strange and snakelike slipped gently around Selby's waist. It was Terrence Tusk's trunk reaching in from the next cage and soon Selby was lifted high in the air.

"I'll take the high road," Selby sang as he was lowered to the safety of the elephant's cage, "and Tina can have the low road. Phew! Thanks Terry. You rescued me just in time. One more minute and that highland fling would have been my last fling."

THE
DIABOLICAL
DISAPPEARING
DOG

It was one of those days when Mrs Trifle would gladly have given someone else the job of being mayor of Bogusville. The day went from catastrophe to catastrophe and crisis to crisis and then — to make matters worse — in dashed international daredevil superstar Awful Knoffle.

"Mrs Mayor, ya gotta give me permission to leap Gumboot Gorge," Awful Knoffle pleaded, holding up a photo of himself jumping seventy-two school buses on his motorcycle. "Nobody's ever done it before. From the moment I saw it I knew I had to be the first. It's just a *gorgeous* gorge. Ha ha ha ha ha."

"I'd hate to have you land in Bogusville Hospital. As I recall you didn't quite make it over the seventy-second school bus and you crashed and broke every bone in your body," Mrs Trifle said.

"Yeah, well, I don't remember much about that but Gumboot Gorge will be a snap. I can do it!" Awful said, pounding the mayor's desk with his fist and hitting her sandwiches by mistake.

"If there was anything I could do to keep you from this crazy scheme of yours, I would," Mrs Trifle said. "But as it happens, Gumboot Gorge isn't in Bogusville so you can do as you like and *I* can't prevent you."

"Aawl riiiiiiight! Why am I wasting my time talking to you then? I've got a gorge to jump!" Awful said, dashing for the door just as Dudley Dewmop, Bogusville's short-sighted, part-time dog-catcher stumbled in.

"I've got him! I finally caught the phantom pooch!" Dudley screamed as he threw a hessian bag with a large lump in it on the carpet. "Every night for weeks I've heard that unmistakable baying — Oooooooooo. Ooooooooooo," Dudley howled at the ceiling. "But I finally caught him with my Handy-Dandy Telescoping Sleeve Net." With this a long pole with a net on the end shot out of his sleeve and captured Mrs Trifle's squashed sandwiches.

"Dudley!" Mrs Trifle said grabbing what was left of the sandwiches from Dudley's net. "What are you talking about and exactly what is in that bag?"

"It's him!" Dudley said, throwing open the bag to reveal a rather embarrassed Selby who wasn't having much of a day either. "The phantom pooch! The mystery mutt! The diabolical disappearing dog that howls in the night and keeps everyone awake! I've caught him!"

"That's no disappearing dog. That's my dog, Selby," Mrs Trifle said. "And he doesn't go out and howl at night. He stays right in my house and sleeps like any normal dog. In the past three weeks you've brought me seventeen perfectly innocent dogs, three cats and a possum and each time you said you'd caught this mysterious dog of yours. Forget the phantom pooch and buy a decent pair of glasses so you can see properly."

"Er … ah … yes, Mrs Mayor," Dudley said, backing out the door and pushing the Sleeve Net up his sleeve again as he listened to a distant sound that could have been the unmistakable baying of the phantom pooch but was really Dr Trifle's new invention, a talking floral clock in the Bogusville Memorial Rose Garden screaming out, "*It's twenty past twooooooooooooo!*"

"Poor Selby," Mrs Trifle said. "I hope the silly man didn't hurt you."

"Hurt, schmurt," thought Selby, whose pride — but nothing much else — was hurt as anyone's might have been if they were netted and dumped on the mayor's carpet. "If that near-sighted ninny catches me again I'll bite him into next week."

All of which he thought too soon because the next day every man and his dog (which included Selby) was at Gumboot Gorge waiting to see Awful Knoffle make his death-defying leap.

"This is great!" said Selby, who loved anything death-defying as long as his own life wasn't at stake, and he climbed a tall tree away from the crowd.

"What a view!" Selby thought as he grabbed thinner and thinner branches near the top of the tree. "From here I'll be able to see Awful tear all the way up the mountain and then leap the gorge."

All of which would have been okay if Selby hadn't spied an even thinner branch at the very top of the tree where the view was even better — which still would have been okay if he hadn't sat on the branch — and which still would have been okay if the branch hadn't decided at that very moment to break off, sending Selby plummeting downward, hitting branch after branch on the way.

"Ooooooooooooh! Noooooooooooo!" Selby screamed, as he landed, slightly bruised, on the ground. Dudley Dewmop, who was innocently admiring Awful Knoffle's roaring motorcycle, heard Selby's scream and mistook it for the unmistakable baying of the phantom pooch.

"It's him! It's the diabolical disappearing dog!" Dudley screamed as he knocked Awful from the motorcycle and hopped on. "I've got to get him!"

Dudley put the big bike in gear and tore up the steep slope towards Selby.

"Gimme my bike back, numbskull!" Awful screamed, chasing after Dudley.

In a flash Selby was on his feet and running, with the motorcycle just behind.

"I've got you now!" yelled the short-sighted part-time dog-catcher.

"Help!" thought Selby as the puzzled crowd watched him tear up and down the steep sides of Gumboot Mountain with the mad motorcyclist hot on his heels. "Somebody's got to stop this (*puff*) madman before he runs me over!"

The answer came to Selby in a flash: "I'll (*puff*) run to the edge of the gorge (*puff*) and he'll have to stop and get off the bike (*puff puff*). Then I'll climb down to where he can't get to me!"

Selby dashed to the edge of the gorge as fast as he could and then dug in his heels for a quick sliding stop.

"Oh, no!" Selby thought as he skidded towards the top of the cliff with the short-sighted motorcyclist just behind. "I'm not going to stop in time! This time I'm really a done dog!"

The crowd screamed as Selby flew out into the middle of the gorge with the motorcycle soaring through the air above him.

"I've got you now, phantom pooch!" Dudley yelled, seeing the blur that was Selby dropping into the gorge and wondering why the ground was suddenly so smooth.

With this, Dudley shot out his Telescoping Sleeve Net and scooped up the airborne dog. Together they tore over the gorge, landing safely on the other side, and screeched to a halt.

"I'm not going to suffer the embarrassment of being dumped on Mrs Trifle's carpet again," Selby thought as he ripped the net apart with his teeth and jumped into the safety of a nearby bush. "It's bad enough that he nearly killed me!"

Dudley threw down the big motorcycle and searched the empty net for his captive as some of the crowd gathered around to congratulate him on the jump he didn't know he'd made.

"I had him but he got away!" Dudley screamed looking at the hole in the net. "The diabolical disappearing dog's done it again! Oh, well, I'd better get this motorcycle back to Awful so he can do his death-defying jump."

"And I'm staying home till that twit buys some new glasses," Selby said, making a Dudley-defying jump out of the bushes and running for town, passing the weeping daredevil as he went.

SELBY'S LUCKY STAR

"Glenda Glitter my favourite movie star is right here in Bogusville!" Selby said as he read in the *Bogusville Banner* that the Tinsel Trust Film Company was at the Bogusville Timber Mill making a movie called *The Perils of Raelene*. "She's so beautiful. I just have to go and watch her act."

Inside the timber mill the movie crew was busy setting up bright lights, cameras and microphones.

"There she is!" Selby thought as he trotted in unnoticed and quickly spotted Glenda, standing on one side as someone sprayed her hair and someone else put powder on her face. "How I'd love to talk to her about her movies."

In a minute the director lifted his loudspeaker and shouted, "Places everyone!" And then, pointing to a huge log that was ready to be sawed down the middle by an enormous, round saw blade, he said, "Glenda, sweetie. Be a nice girl and hop up on that log."

"Log?" Glenda said looking at the gigantic tree trunk. "Oh, no you don't. I'm not climbing up on that thing. And nobody's going to make me!"

"What a voice! What passion!" Selby thought. "I've been in love with her ever since I saw her in that dreadful movie, *Kelpie, King of Queensland*. She only had one line to say but she said it beautifully."

"You have to. It's in the script," the director said. "This is the scene where you're tied to the log while the saw cuts it down the middle. Preston and Rex fight and you scream your little blonde head off. When Preston wins the fight he runs over and pulls the lever to stop the saw. Got it?"

"It's too dangerous and I'm not going to do it!" Glenda said, flashing her lavender eyes and throwing her hair over her shoulder the way movie stars do. "You can get someone else!"

"Shut up, Glenda!" the director yelled. "Just do as I say!"

"That's no way to get the greatest actress in Australia to do what you want," Selby thought angrily. "She could just walk away and never finish the movie."

"What if Preston loses the fight?" Glenda asked, climbing up a ladder and onto the log while two men tied her down with a thick rope. "I mean, he might get knocked down. What if he doesn't get up in time to stop the saw? What'll happen to me?"

"Actors don't really fight in a movie. You ought to know that. They'll just pretend to punch each other," the director said. "Besides, there are plenty of us here to pull the lever and stop the saw if anything goes wrong."

"You'd better be right," Glenda said. "I don't fancy being sliced down the middle."

"Action!" the director yelled and Rex and Preston pretended to fight as the saw sliced its way down the log, throwing up a cloud of sawdust. "Cut! I mean, stop! The fighting looks too phoney. Pull the log back and try it again."

Again and again they shot the scene until Glenda was so hoarse from screaming that she could barely talk.

"This is great!" Selby thought, squeezing through the crowd to get a better view. "What wonderful acting!"

"Ouch! Stop that!" Preston cried, clutching his jaw. "You're not supposed to *really* hit me!"

"I only tapped you. It was an accident!" Rex yelled. "Can I help it if I made a mistake? Don't be such a baby!"

"Don't you call me a baby, you big sissy!" Preston yelled.

"I am not a sissy!"

"Yes you are!"

"Am not!"

"Are too!"

"Am not!"

"Gentlemen! Gentlemen!" the director yelled, holding them apart. "I think we're all a bit tired. Let's take a short break for coffee and then we'll do the scene one last time. Everyone but you," he said looking up at Glenda. "You stay up on the log. It's too hard getting you down and then tying you on the log again.

46

Have a rest. You must be tired after all that screaming."

In two minutes the film crew had left the shed and Glenda was fast asleep and snoring.

"This is my chance to get a really close look at her," Selby thought as he climbed up the rope and stared at the glamorous star.

"What beautiful skin," Selby said. "And what gorgeous hair. I remember the way it looked when she played Princess Su in *Raid on Planet Kapon*. I can see why actors are always falling in love with her and fighting over her. And here I am (*sigh*) alone with her."

Selby wrapped the rope tightly around one paw so he wouldn't fall and then leaned down and pressed his lips lightly on her cheek, covering them with make-up.

"Crumbs," Selby said, taking a breath and getting a lungful of powder. "Ah-choo!" he screamed, losing his balance and thrashing about in the air with a hind leg. "Ah-choo! Ah-double-choooooo!"

Selby's leg swung around and caught the lever, knocking it over out of reach and starting the great saw blade whirring.

"What's happening?" Glenda said looking up at Selby. "Are we shooting again? Hey! Where did the dog come from? There's no dog in the script. What's going on here?! Where is everybody?"

"Crikey," Selby thought, desperately trying to untangle his paw from the rope. "I've started the flippin' saw and now I can't reach the lever to stop it."

The whirring blade sliced its way down the

log towards Glenda who screamed louder and louder.

"If she'd only stop pulling on the rope I could get my leg loose," Selby thought. "If I don't get out of here fast, we'll both be sliced salami!"

"Help! Save me!" Glenda screamed louder than she had when the cameras were going.

"I've got to tell her to stop struggling," Selby thought as the saw sped towards Glenda's head. "But if I talk to her my (*gulp*) secret will be out. And if my secret gets out, scientists will want to study me, the only talking dog in Australia and — for all I know — in the world. They'll keep me in a laboratory and ask me stupid questions all day long (*gulp*). I'd rather be dead than let people know that I'm a talking, thinking, feeling dog. Yipes!" Selby thought suddenly. "Did I say *dead*?"

Selby looked deep in Glenda's lavender eyes and said suddenly in plain English, "Listen carefully, Glenda. There's no time to lose."

"Hey," Glenda said. "You talked. The dog talked! How is that possible? The only talking dog I ever saw was the dog in my picture,

Kelpie, King of Queensland, and he wasn't really a talking dog. They used the director's voice. In fact —"

"Shut up, Glenda," Selby said sternly. "Just do as I say! Stay still and stop struggling!"

Glenda was so stunned by the sight of a talking dog that she stayed still for a moment and Selby jerked his foot loose.

"Now there's some slack in the rope! Squiggle over to the side of the log, Glenda!" Selby yelled. "Quick!"

The saw caught Glenda's blonde wig and ripped it to shreds just as she squiggled, leaving her dangling on one side of the log and Selby on the other. As the blade passed between them it cut the rope and they fell safely to the floor.

"I don't know who you are or how you learned to talk," Glenda said, throwing her arms around Selby and giving him a big kiss on the lips, "but you must be the smartest, bravest dog in the whole world. How would you like to be in one of my movies? They're making a sequel to *Kelpie, King of Queensland*."

"I — I — don't think so," Selby stammered.

"What's going on in there?" the director yelled as he ran into the shed just as Selby was running out. "And whose dog is that?"

"I don't know whose dog he is and I don't care," Glenda said dreamily. "All I can say is, he's twice the dog you'll ever be."

THE SCREAMING MIMIS

"Bushfire love, yeah yeah, bushfire love," Selby sang along with the latest video clip by the rock super-group, The Screaming Mimis, as he danced around in front of the TV. "That Mimi, the lead singer, is great! And, what's more, the group is coming to Bogusville tonight! I've got to find a way to get into the Town Hall to see them!"

That night Selby ran down to the Bogusville Town Hall just in time to see *The Screaming Mimis* unloading the equipment from their van. He looked around for a way into the hall but there were guards at every entrance holding back screaming fans.

"If only I could get by the guards and then hide under a table till the show starts," Selby thought as he watched the band come and go through a back door. "How will I do it?"

For a moment, everyone was in the hall and Selby jumped in the back of the van.

"Hmmmmmmmm. What's this?" he said, pulling at the sides of a big wooden box. "They must have equipment stored in it. If I can only get in it . . ."

The box was nailed shut but some of the nails had come loose and Selby prised the side open and hopped in, hitting a mass of wires.

"Phew!" he said, pulling the side closed again after him. "There's barely enough room in here for me." He was peering out through the tiny holes in the sides of the box when Mimi and her drummer, Slam-Bam Benson got in the back of the van.

"Help me carry the box, Slam-Bam," Mimi, said in a tiny, high-pitched voice.

"Cripes!" Selby thought. "That's Mimi. But what's happened to her voice? She doesn't sound anything like her records."

Mimi and Slam-Bam lifted the box out of the van and began carrying it inside.

Suddenly Mimi put her end of the box down.

"I can't take it any more!" she blurted out. "Driving all day, working all night — we've been on the road for six months and it's just too much! I can't sing tonight. I can't!"

"Please, Mimi. We can't go on without you," Slam-Bam pleaded. "It's the last night of the tour. We can't cancel on our last night."

"I don't care. I sound like a budgie," Mimi said, wiping away a tear. "If I don't sing *Bushfire Love* at the top of my voice, the audience will feel cheated. And I can't do it."

"Don't worry," Slam-Bam said. "We'll turn the amps way up."

"It won't be enough," Mimi said. "Listen to me. I can hardly talk."

"Speak up, I can hardly hear you," Slam-Bam said.

"I *am* speaking up," Mimi said in a voice not much louder than a whisper.

"Don't worry, Mimi," Slam-Bam reassured her. "We live in the age of electronic wizardry. We'll turn the amps way up and that'll do till we get to *Bushfire Love*. Then we'll connect up the Super Computerised High-Pitched Ear-Piercing Brain-Scrambling Sound Blaster. It'll make a whisper sound like a stick of gelignite."

"I don't know..." Mimi started.

"Trust me, Mimi. I built it myself and I tell you it can do everything except sit up and sing," Slam-Bam said, "and I'm working on that."

"Wow!" Selby thought. "A Super Computerised High-Pitched Ear-Piercing Brain-Scrambling Sound Blaster! I can't wait to hear it."

"No offence, Slam-Bam, but I don't trust it. We haven't used it before in a concert," Mimi said as she peered down into the holes in the box, not quite seeing the dog-figure lurking in the darkness inside. "Besides, it's been bouncing around in the van so long, it's falling apart. Look, the nails are coming out."

"That's nothing. I can fix that in a second," Slam-Bam said.

And before Selby could say, "Oh no, I've just climbed into a Super Computerised High-Pitched Ear-Piercing Brain-Scrambling Sound Blaster without realising it," Slam-Bam dropped his end of the blaster and gave the loose nails a whack or two with his hammer — which would have been okay if Selby's head hadn't been right up against the side of the box and got such a good banging that he didn't remember a thing till three paragraphs from now.

"There, it's fixed," Slam-Bam said. "It'll really blast the rafters, you wait and see."

"I warn you, Slam-Bam," Mimi peeped. "If it doesn't work tonight, I'll put an axe through it."

Selby awoke that evening to the deafening sound of drums and screaming teenagers. He peered out through the holes and saw the flicker of lasers in the air.

"Now for our final song," Mimi squeaked as she connected up the sound blaster. "*Bushfire Love!*"

"Oh, no!" Selby thought as he peered out of the blaster and then scratched and pushed with all his might. "If I don't get out of here fast, this

Super Computerised High-Pitched Ear-Piercing Brain-Scrambling Sound Blaster's going to pierce my ears and scramble my brains for sure!"

Slam-Bam hit a drum and Selby bounced off the inside of the blaster, his fur standing on end, then collapsed in a heap, his ears ringing like churchbells.

"I've got to do something fast!" Selby thought. "If he hits that drum again, I'm gone! My secret doesn't matter any more. It's a matter of life and death! Help!" Selby screamed in plain English at the top of his lungs. "There's a talking dog stuck in the sound blaster — and it's me! Let me out!"

But Selby's screams were nothing but a peep as the drummer sent another and another beat through the blaster.

"I've got to destroy this contraption before it destroys me!" Selby thought as he grabbed a mouthful of wires and pulled them, covering himself in a shower of sparks.

"That's done it!" he thought. "I've disconnected the blaster. Now all I have to do is wait till someone opens it."

Mimi sang soundlessly for a second and then gave the blaster a whopping great thump with her boot.

"I told you it wouldn't work!" she cried. "It's a useless piece of junk."

With this she grabbed a fire axe and raised it over her head, ready to chop the blaster in two.

"Gulp," Selby said, staring up at the axe. "This is not the way I wanted the blaster to be opened. I've got to do something before that crazy crooner gives me the chop!"

And with this he screamed out the chorus to

Bushfire Love as loud as he could, imitating Mimi's voice:

> *"Ain't cryin' out for you no mo'*
> *My love is burnin' on a ten mile front*
> *Clearin' a firebreak with my eyes*
> *You are the backburn of my heart.*
> *Bushfire love, yeah yeah*
> *Bushfire love . . . "*

Mimi stared at the blaster as Selby sang on and on, louder and louder.

"I can't believe it," she said, scratching her head. "That box is singing my song!"

Selby finished the song to a roar of applause. And before he realised what he was doing, he took a deep bow, sending the blaster tumbling off the stage and onto the darkness of the dance floor below, where it broke open.

"I can't believe it," Slam-Bam said. "I said that contraption could do everything but sit up and sing. I was wrong — it sat up and sang."

"And in quite a good voice," Selby said as he ran across the crowded dance floor and out the exit. "Even if I do say so myself."

FAMOUS DEAD POETS

Selby was feeling guilty. He was feeling guilty in the way a dog might feel guilty if a crowd of crazy poetry lovers had ripped apart an old mansion and he had found out that it was all his fault. The reason he was feeling this way was that a crowd of crazy poetry lovers *had* ripped apart an old mansion and it *was* all his fault.

"I don't deserve to be their dog," Selby thought as he looked up at Dr and Mrs Trifle. "They're such warm and wonderful people and I'm such a ... such a ... well they'd never forgive me if they knew what I'd done."

Selby curled up on the carpet and put his

paws over his eyes, thinking of the day before
— the day it had all begun ...

It was evening and he and the Trifles were
sitting in front of the TV set watching an
episode of *Famous Dead Poets*.

Malcolm Mumbles, the narrator of the
program, was walking along the beach at Surfers
Paradise reciting a poem by the famous dead
surfie poet, Clancy of the Undertow:

"The waves, the waves
I'll not forget —
I don't know when
I've been so wet.
I wouldn't want to place a bet
The waves won't get me yet —
Unless a shark gets me first."

"He was doing okay till the last line," Dr Trifle said. "All those *forgets*, *wets*, *bets* and *yets* but then up pops a *first* and it doesn't rhyme. What sort of poetry is that, dear?"

"It's the kind of poetry they write these days," Mrs Trifle said. "It sort of rhymes but, on the other hand, it sort of doesn't. It's much easier to write."

"It's dreadful if you ask me," Selby thought knowing that no one was about to ask him.

"Next we have a not-so-famous dead poet named Whittlebone Jones," Malcolm Mumbles said, sitting on a frisky horse in a dry riverbed and trying to face the camera as the horse turned in circles. "He lived in the days when poetry rhymed all the way through. He spent his life roaming the outback, appearing at drovers' campfires. He'd ask for a mug of tea and a chunk of damper and then he'd recite his poetry before disappearing again."

Malcolm Mumbles' horse darted away for a second and then galloped back to the camera.

"We know that Whittlebone Jones wrote a lot of poetry," Malcolm Mumbles said with a little bit of panic in his voice, "but all of it is lost except one poem. And that's the one that tells of the tragic accident that ended his roaming. It goes like this:

'I rode onto a silvery plain,
The sun was setting o'er the cane,
I rode through grass and rode through gorse,
And then, alas, fell off my horse.'"

"Not a great poem," Mrs Trifle said.

"Maybe that's why he's not-so-famous," Dr Trifle said, "instead of just plain famous."

"Well, he deserves to be more famous than Clancy of the Undertow," Mrs Trifle said. "Even if there's only one of his poems left."

"We know very little about the last years of Whittlebone Jones," Malcolm Mumbles said over his shoulder as the horse turned around again. "We only know that he lived out his final years in this house," he added, holding up a photograph of an old house. "We don't know where the house is, which is a pity because the lost manuscripts of Whittlebone Jones are probably hidden there somewhere."

"With any luck they'll stay lost," Selby thought as the horse threw Malcolm Mumbles into the riverbed. "But hold the show! Galloping galahs! That house is Bunya–Bunya Breezes! I'd recognise that funny-shaped chimney anywhere!" Selby thought, remembering the photo of the house that Mrs Trifle had on her desk in the folder marked *New Recreation Centre*. "That's the empty house down the street. It's the one the council is going to turn into a recreation centre."

An hour later when the Trifles went out for a walk, Selby phoned Malcolm Mumbles.

"I saw your program today, Mal," Selby said, "and I just wanted to tell you that I know where Whittlebone Jones' house is. It's an empty house right at the end of my street. What's the reward?"

"Who said anything about a reward?" Malcolm Mumbles asked nastily.

"Well ... *I* did," Selby said, trying not to be nasty back. "If I tell you where the house is and you find the lost manuscripts, you'll be a rich man. It's only fair that I should get a reward."

"The manuscripts are not worth anything," Malcolm said. "I only want them for the sentimental value."

"Well if that's the case I'll find them myself," Selby said, knowing that he couldn't because his paws weren't suited to taking apart floors and walls to look for lost manuscripts, "and keep all the sentimental value for myself. Goodbye."

"Hold on!" Malcolm yelled. "Just a minute! Okay, okay, I'll see about a reward. Just give me your name and address and we'll send you … we'll see what we can send you."

"Just send the reward to Mr S. Trifle," Selby said, "at Bunya-Bunya Crescent in Bogusville. I'm at number —"

"So Whittlebone Jones' house is at the end of Bunya-Bunya Crescent in Bogusville!" Malcolm Mumbles screamed.

"I didn't say that," Selby said.

"Yes you did! You said it was at the end of your street and you said you live in Bunya-Bunya Crescent," Malcolm Mumbles said. "You also said the house was empty! Even Blind Freddy could find it from those clues! So long, you mug, I'm going to find the lost manuscripts of Whittlebone Jones!"

"He tricked me," Selby said, wondering if Blind Freddy was a little-known dead poet or a famous one. "But I know what I'll do. As soon as the sun is up I'll nip down to Bunya-Bunya Breezes and start looking. *He* has to come all the way from the city. I'll beat him to it."

Early next morning Selby approached Bunya-Bunya Breezes and heard the sounds of ripping and banging. Inside was a mob of people pulling the old house apart looking for the lost manuscripts.

"Crikey!" Selby thought. "They're wrecking the new recreation centre." And before he could stop himself he'd yelled out, "Stop it at once! Stop this madness!"

Suddenly the ripping and banging stopped and Malcolm Mumbles poked his head out a window.

"Who said that?" he asked, seeing only a dog with a purple face. "Okay, back to work everybody."

"Mrs Trifle will be furious. I've got to stop them," Selby thought, "even if it means talking and (*gulp*) giving away my secret!"

But just then there was a great cracking noise and the roof began to fall in.

"Everybody out!" Malcolm Mumbles yelled and poetry lovers dived out windows and jumped through holes in the walls till the last boards had fallen and Bunya-Bunya Breezes lay in ruins.

"We looked everywhere," Malcolm said with tears in his eyes. "They weren't in the walls or the ceilings or in the floors or even in the dirt under the house. The lost manuscripts are still lost."

"And so am I," Selby said, slinking off home. "It's all my fault. They destroyed the new recreation centre because of me. I don't deserve to live with such wonderful people as Dr and Mrs Trifle. I'm just not worthy of them. I'll have to tell them what happened. It doesn't matter that I'll be their servant for life. I don't even deserve to be their slave."

And Selby was feeling so guilty as he lay there on the carpet looking up at the Trifles that he was about to say, "All right, enough's enough. I, Selby, your unworthy dog, am able to talk as well as the next man," when Mrs Trifle picked up the photograph of Bunya–Bunya Breezes and looked at it.

"It's a pity," she said. "It was the last house around here with one of those funny-shaped chimneys, and now it's gone. A hundred years ago all the houses in the bush had them."

"Crumbs," Selby thought. "I thought it *had* to be Whittlebone Jones' house because of the chimney and now I find out that there were houses like that all over the country. Things are getting worse by the minute."

"It had to go anyway," Dr Trifle said, "to make way for the new recreation centre that's going to be built. We should be thankful that it didn't cost anything to have it torn down."

"Yes," Mrs Trifle said, not seeing Selby's ears prick up, "it was good of Malcolm Mumbles to help us out. I don't know why he did it but I think I'll ask the council if we can name the new recreation centre The Malcolm Mumbles Sports and Leisure Centre."

"Yes," said Dr Trifle. "What a good idea."

"Life's just not fair," Selby thought as he trotted off for his evening's walk. "That recreation centre ought to be named after me. Besides, Selby's Sports and Leisure Centre even sounds better."

SELBY SOARS TO NEW HEIGHTS

"Galloping galaxies!" cried Dr Trifle's old friend and amateur astronomer, Percy Peach, as he peered through the doctor's brand new binocular bilateral super close-up tracking telescope which poked up through a huge hole in the Trifles' garage roof. "Either there's dust on your telescope or a tiny piece of Haydee's Comet just broke away when it rounded Mars! Have a look!"

"It's hopeless trying to show me," said Dr Trifle, nearly asleep in his chair and wondering how astronomers managed to stay up all night to study the stars. "I never should have built that silly telescope. All I ever see is eyelashes: gigantic blinking eyelashes. The sky is full of them."

"It's right near Sirius, the Dog Star. I'll calculate where it's going," Percy, who hated calculators and biros, said as he whipped out a pad of paper, a bottle of ink and a quill pen.

Percy began scribbling lines and lines of letters and columns and columns of numbers at great speed and then throwing the papers on the floor where Selby lay trying to sleep.

"What a pity. It seems our new comet is going to zoom off harmlessly into space," Percy said to the nearly-sleeping Dr Trifle. "I had hoped it would come crashing into the atmosphere and make lots of pretty streaks and light up the sky like Cracker Night, the way comets do sometimes. Could you please check my calculations while I climb up on the roof to make sure it wasn't just on the telescope?"

"Poor Dr Trifle needs his sleep," Selby said, waking up and stretching and seeing that Dr Trifle was finally asleep in his chair and that Percy Peach had gone. "That Percy kept him awake too long. It's not good for him. Hmmmmmmmmmmmmmm. Oh, good! Now's my chance to look through Dr Trifle's new telescope."

Selby ran to the telescope and peeped up through it, not seeing eyelashes — because he didn't have any — but seeing instead a gigantic head that looked like some sort of monster from the *Revolt of the Universe* movies.

"Aaaaarrrrrgggggh!" screamed Selby at the sight of Percy.

"Aaaaarrrrrgggggh!" screamed Percy back as he saw Selby's tiny eyes peering up at him.

And before Selby realised that it was only Percy checking the telescope for dust, he jumped backwards, knocking over the inkwell — all of which would have been okay if he hadn't got a tiny drop of ink on one toenail.

"You frightened the life out of me!" Percy screamed at Dr Trifle who was now waking up and wondering what all the screaming was about. "I saw your eyes in the telescope and thought you were some sort of monster."

"Am I?" Dr Trifle asked, still wondering what was happening.

"Of course you're not. Don't be silly," Percy said, gathering together all the papers in one big clump and thrusting them into Dr Trifle's hands. "There's no dust on your telescope. This can only mean one thing."

"What?" Dr Trifle said, rubbing his eyes and not really listening to anything his old friend was saying.

"That a tiny piece of Haydee's Comet has broken away and become a comet itself," Percy said. "Don't you ever listen to anything I say? Never mind. Just check my calculations and see if I'm right that the new comet is going to miss the earth altogether."

Dr Trifle looked over the lines and lines of letters and columns and columns of numbers.

"Ahah! I think you've gone wrong here. You missed a number on your second last page," Dr Trifle said, pointing to the ragged number 1 that looked more like a dog's inky toenail print than a real number 1. "In fact if we recalculate you'll see this little comet is just about to zoop straight down to earth!" Dr Trifle said, finishing the calculation on his pocket calculator. "Not only to earth but directly to Bogusville! It should light up the sky like Cracker Night!"

"Heavenly bodies!" Percy Peach screamed as he studied the number 1 he'd missed and noticed how much it looked like a dog's-toenail-dipped-in-ink mark. "We're in the perfect position to see it. We'll get the best view of anyone on earth! They'll have to name it after us! It'll be called the Peach–Trifle Comet! There's no time to lose! You look through one of these eyepieces and I'll look through the other. Before the night is out, the comet will be here and we'll be famous!"

"Cripes!" Selby thought as he crept out of the garage to his favourite hiding place: the garden shed. "Now poor Dr Trifle's going to stay up all night looking for a comet that isn't even coming towards earth. And it's all my fault for stepping in that ink. Oh, woe woe woe. I wish he'd just forget all about it and go to bed. If only I could think of something. If only a brilliant idea would pop into my brain. Hmmmmmmmmmmm."

Selby climbed through the hole in the garden shed.

"I've got it!" he cried as a brilliant idea popped into his brain. "I've got it!"

Selby lifted box after box off the shelves in front of him till he found one labelled, "Left-over Sparklers from Cracker Night".

"I think I've just found the Peach–Trifle Comet!" Selby said, grabbing a sparkler from the box.

Selby climbed quietly up onto the garage and peeked down through a crack in the roof to see the two men, each peering up through a different nocular of the binocular bilateral super close-up tracking telescope.

"All I have to do is light this sparkler and hold it in my teeth and then make a comet-like leap over the end of the telescope," Selby thought as he lit the sparkler and made a perfect comet-like leap over the telescope.

"That's it!" Percy screamed. "Did you see it?"

"I'm sorry," Dr Trifle said sleepily. "All I saw was eyelashes."

"Well *I* saw it so now they'll have to name it after me!" Percy said. "What a sight! But you know," he added, scratching his head the way astronomers do when they're thinking,

"there was something odd about the Peach Comet."

"What was that?" Dr Trifle asked.

"It made a comet-like streak across the sky in the usual way but I think I also saw something else. If I'm not mistaken I saw the faint image of a dog's face."

"Sirius?" Dr Trifle asked.

"Of course I'm serious," said Percy.

"No, I mean Sirius, the Dog Star. That must have been what you saw," Dr Trifle said to the puzzled Percy as he headed off to bed to get some sleep at last.

"The Dog Star," Selby thought as he curled up to get some sleep too. "That's me all right."

THE STAR OF LAHTIDOH

The night the world famous opera singer, Dame Lily Larinks, came to town dripping with the most expensive jewellery, there was a reception at the Town Hall and everyone who was anyone (and in Bogusville that was everyone) was there. Some came to see the famous singer sing a few songs and talk about her life in opera, but most Bogusvillians weren't opera fans. In fact they were a little suspicious of singers who didn't play along on the guitar as they sang — which Dame Lily didn't. No, they came to see the blinding sparkle of the Star of Lahtidoh, the biggest diamond in the world, which hung on a thin gold chain around the great woman's neck.

It was the hottest evening of the year and Selby would have happily stayed at home to watch *Inspector Quigley's Casebook*, his favourite TV detective show, but he too was dying for a glimpse of the glittering gem.

"Is it true that there's a curse on the Star?" Mrs Trifle asked Dame Lily as she dipped another cup of orange-lime cordial from a punchbowl so packed with ice-cubes that a few tumbled to the floor.

"There's a lot of talk about a curse," Dame Lily said in a singsong voice, "because of what's happened to the owners of the gem. You see, it was found by an explorer in Africa. He tripped on it and broke his toe. When a doctor came to help him he unfortunately gave the explorer the wrong medicine and he died. But it was lucky for the doctor because he kept the Star in payment for his services and became a very rich man. Sadly, he was run over accidentally by his own limousine in London some years later. The chauffeur felt terrible about it but, happily, he inherited the gem and became very rich for a time."

"And what happened to him?" Mrs Trifle asked.

"He and his family drowned when their yacht sank off the coast of Italy."

"How terrible."

"Yes, the only survivor was a simple young deckhand who rowed the lifeboat into port the next day and told of the terrible storm," Dame Lily said. "Apparently the only thing he was able to rescue was the Star of Lahtidoh."

"And did you buy the Star from him?" Mrs Trifle asked.

"Good heavens no," Dame Lily said. "I married him. He was my first husband. So you see, I don't believe in the curse. I just think that the previous owners had a run of dreadfully bad luck."

"Sounds like more than just bad luck," thought Selby, catching an ice-cube in his mouth as it fell from the punchbowl. "But what a beautiful diamond! The sparkles are all different colours like hundreds and thousands."

"What I will say for the Star," Dame Lily said, "is that I believe it has magical powers."

"Magical powers?" Mrs Trifle asked. "Do you really?"

"Yes, I do. It certainly has a mind of its own. Twice I've misplaced it and both times it told me, through my feelings, where it was."

"A mind of its own?" Selby thought as another ice-cube fell to the floor and he caught it on the first bounce. "Some people will believe anything."

"Is it insured?" Dr Trifle asked as he rubbed his sweating forehead with a handful of ice. "In case it's lost — or stolen?"

"I'm afraid it's not," Dame Lily said. "The Star is worth squillions. No one could ever insure it. It's worth more than a whole insurance company. I have guards instead. They keep watch on it every second of the day."

"That's funny," Mrs Trifle said, "I don't see any guards."

"Hmmmmmmm, how curious," Dame Lily said, looking around the hall. "I wonder where they've gone. Well I don't think we have to worry about jewel thieves in a little town like this, do we? Ha ha ha."

Selby looked around through a forest of legs as he sucked another ice-cube, but only saw people who lived in Bogusville.

"'Show me a peaceful town,'" Selby thought, quoting the words of Inspector Quigley from the episode called *A Peaceful Town*, "'and I will show you a place where a crime is just waiting to happen.'"

Just then Selby saw a couple of suspicious men in suits making their way towards the famous opera singer.

"Out of the way!" one of them said as he pushed forward.

Selby stopped sucking and started staring. "Crumbs!" he thought, seeing the bulge in the man's coat that could only have been a pistol. "This is it — a crime just waiting to happen! They're international jewel thieves and they've captured the guards and tied them up in a back room somewhere so they can steal the Star of Lahtidoh! I've got to stop them!"

The men came closer and Selby — remembering how Inspector Quigley outwitted a roomful of spies in *The Roomful of Spies* — ran for the light switch, casting the room into darkness.

"Don't move!" one of the men yelled and he fired his pistol in the air which made everyone move very fast in every direction.

"They're after the Star!" Selby cried out in plain English as he bumped his way across the crowded room accidentally knocking all the people down who hadn't already fallen down. "Dame Lily! Hide the diamond, quick!"

Selby dashed about trying to find Dame Lily. Finally a shaft of moonlight caught the Star of Lahtidoh which still hung from the woman's neck. Remembering the way the archvillain trained a dog to steal jewellery in the Inspector Quigley episode called *The Doggie Done It Diamond Caper*, Selby leapt up and snatched the gem in his teeth, flinging it high in the air.

The lights came back on just as Selby crashed to the floor, hitting his head.

"It's gone!" Dame Lily sang in full soprano. "The diamond is gone!"

"The dog took it!" one of the suspicious men — who were really the guards and who had snuck out to see the latest episode of *Inspector Quigley's Casebook* but who couldn't find a TV — said as he pounced on Selby and pulled his mouth open. "He's swallowed it, just like in *The Doggie Done It Diamond Caper*. If we don't get it back we'll be out of a job!"

"You'll be out of *two* jobs!" Dame Lily, who was good at maths, screeched.

"We'll just have to wait till the diamond comes out naturally," the first guard said, looking at Selby who was still dazed by the bump on the head.

"We can't wait!" the other one said, reaching for a cake knife and raising it in the air over Selby's stomach. "We have to find out right now if the diamond's in him."

"They can't (*gulp*) do this to me!" thought Selby, suddenly realising the terrible mistake he'd made as the dagger descended. "Or can they ... ? But wait! My only chance is to scream out in plain English. But if I do that, my secret will be out! Oh, no!"

Selby was about to speak when Mrs Trifle suddenly stepped forward.

"Unhand that dog!" she said, pulling the guard away from Selby and giving him a good shake. "He is innocent of any wrongdoing. It's all been a terrible mistake! The diamond is probably on the floor somewhere, mixed up with all this ice!"

The guests searched frantically for the diamond, checking the ice-cubes that lay all around and throwing them over their shoulders when they'd finished checking them — all of which made things more confusing than ever and looked like a hailstorm had hit the hall.

"Stop!" Dame Lily yelled after the ice had melted from all the handling and there was still no diamond. "I have a feeling! The Star is trying to tell me where it is! I think it's up there," she said, pointing to the chandelier.

The guards jumped up on the table and started pulling glass bits off the chandelier and throwing them every which way until there was only one left, hanging from a thin gold chain.

"My diamond!" Dame Lily said, snatching the gem and putting it around her neck. "The Star must have sensed danger and shot up to the chandelier where it knew it would be safe. You see, it *does* have a mind of its own."

"I'm getting out of here," Selby thought as he dashed out of the hall towards home to see the last part of *Inspector Quigley's Casebook*, his face still red from embarrassment, "before there are any more shooting stars!"

TRYING TO DIET BUT DYING TO TRY IT

Selby was starving.

"He hasn't eaten anything for two days," Mrs Trifle said to Dr Trifle as she topped up Selby's bowl with Chunk-O-Gravy Hunks and added a couple of Dry-Mouth Dog Biscuits. "I'm worried about him."

"I wish she wouldn't worry about me," Selby thought as he watched Dr Trifle who was painting a watercolour portrait of Mrs Trifle for the council chambers.

"Don't worry about Selby," Dr Trifle said as he dabbed at the eyes in his painting with a long paintbrush. "He's just not hungry. It doesn't mean anything. It would be good if he lost some weight, anyway."

"I suppose you're right," Mrs Trifle said. "He's stopped eating before. In fact he did it on my last birthday and on the birthday before, too."

"Come to think of it, it's very odd. Every time you have a birthday we get takeaway food from The Spicy Onion Restaurant, just as we're going to do tonight," Dr Trifle said mentioning their favourite fancy food restaurant. "And whenever we get takeaway food from The Spicy Onion, we get an order of prawns cooked in peanut sauce just for Selby. And Selby *loves* peanut prawns. He'll eat them. You just wait and see."

"Hmmmmmmmm," Mrs Trifle said as she looked over Dr Trifle's shoulder at her portrait. "It's almost as though he knew he was going to get peanut prawns and he stopped eating so that he'd enjoy them more."

"Too right," Selby thought as he closed his eyes so he wouldn't see the Chunk-O-Gravy Hunks and Dry-Mouth Dog Biscuits in his bowl. "It's the only decent food I get all year. I just can't wait till dinnertime."

"My goodness! I'm cross-eyed," Mrs Trifle said suddenly.

"There, there," Dr Trifle said not listening to Mrs Trifle. "I love you just the same and that's all that matters."

"I don't mean my *real* eyes, silly."

"You don't?"

"Of course not," Mrs Trifle said. "My eyes in the painting are crossed."

"My word. So they are," Dr Trifle said, quickly painting them out and repainting them so that now they looked off in different directions.

"I don't think they're quite right, dear."

"Maybe I could paint you with sunglasses on," Dr Trifle said thoughtfully as he changed the eyes again and made them cross-eyed once more. "But it might look a bit odd, I mean all those portraits of mayors of Bogusville hung side by side in the council chambers and you the only one wearing sunglasses."

"Isn't it time for you to pick up the order from The Spicy Onion, dear?" Mrs Trifle said. "You can work on the painting tomorrow."

★ ★ ★

An hour later, the Trifles were about to eat. Before them on the table were some of their favourite fancy foods: barbecued oysters in mango sauce, pickled baby bamboo shoots with bacon rinds and, of course, prawns in peanut sauce for Selby. Just then there was a knock at the door.

"Thornie!" Dr Trifle said, welcoming his cousin Thornton. "What brings you to Bogusville?"

"I've just been to the launching of my new healthy eating book, *Eat For Goodness Sake*, at the third annual Healthy Eating Book Convention and I thought I'd drop in on my way back to the city and bring you some healthy foods," Thornton said, dashing in and putting a bag of food on the dining table.

"Won't you join us?" Mrs Trifle said, raising a forkful of barbecued oysters in mango sauce to her lips.

"What a wonderful idea," said Thornton who had thought of it two hours before. "But wait a minute? What's that muck you're about to eat?"

"That's — that's —" Mrs Trifle began.

Thornton grabbed Mrs Trifle's plate and began poking at it with a finger.

"It looks like barbecued oysters in mango sauce!" he screeched.

"It is," Mrs Trifle said. "Would you like some?"

"I've never seen such an unhealthy combination!" Thornton said, dumping it in the garbage. "And what's that?" he said, grabbing Dr Trifle's plate just as Dr Trifle was trying to rescue it.

"It's — it's —" Dr Trifle started.

"It looks to me like pickled baby bamboo shoots with bacon rinds," Thornton said, throwing the contents of the plate out the window and into the flowerbed. "That's not food, it's fertiliser! It's worse than what your wife was about to eat."

"But — but — but —" Dr Trifle stammered as Thornton filled his plate with wheat germ and buttermilk.

"Now that's good for you. Eat up," Thornton said, filling Mrs Trifle's plate with yoghurt and sultanas. "Remember that Bogusville has an unhealthy climate and you have to eat properly if you want to stay healthy and happy."

"But — but — but —" Mrs Trifle said, not feeling very happy at the moment.

"I can see that I've arrived just in the nick of time," Thornton said. "You're both so weak that you're losing the ability to talk. My goodness! What are you feeding your dog?"

Selby was in the kitchen, wondering why the Trifles had so many crazy relatives and about to take his first mouthful of peanut prawns, when Thornton burst in and tipped Selby's bowl into the garbage.

"Your dog is too fat," Thornton announced to the Trifles. "What he needs to do is to go completely without food for a few days. Now eat up, you two, and then we'll go for a jog."

That night after Thornton and the Trifles were sound asleep Selby still lay clutching his rumbling stomach.

"Oh, the pain, the pain," he thought as he imagined bowls of peanut prawns and even Chunk-O-Gravy Hunks and Dry-Mouth Dog Biscuits. "I can't go without food any longer. If that twit doesn't leave soon I'll die of starvation!" Suddenly a little light went on in Selby's head. "I wonder," he thought. "What if Thornton got sick? I reckon the first thing he'd do is hop in his car and tear back to the healthy climate he came from. But he's not about to get sick, is he?" Selby asked himself. "With all that wheat germ and yoghurt he'll probably live to be a hundred and fifty. Hmmmmmmm. He's not going to get really sick but what if he *thinks* he's sick?"

Selby grabbed a copy of Thornton's book, *Eat For Goodness Sake*, and turned to the section on food and health. There he found a chapter called "Splotches, Blotches and Blots".

"Let's see now," Selby said. "It says here that spots on the side of the nose are a symptom of ... hmmmmmmm."

Selby grabbed Mr Trifle's watercolour set and tore to Thornton's bedroom. He got out the brush and painted three big blue spots on either side of the sleeping man's nose.

The next morning, Thornton woke the Trifles at six o'clock.

"I'm going," he said. "I've got to start work on my new book. Thanks for everything and *stay healthy.*"

"But — but — but —" Mrs Trifle said, handing Thornton a mirror so he could see the spots on his nose.

Thornton grabbed the mirror. "Oh, no! I'm sick!" he screamed. "This is the first stage of bilateral-trispecular-proboscal-everything-itis!"

"Is there a cure for bilateral-trispecular-proboscal-everything-itis?" Dr Trifle asked.

"Raw vegetables, and rest," Thornton said, throwing a bunch of carrots in the blender. "I'll have to stay here for a few weeks till I'm better. I might get worse if I left now."

"I've gone and done it this time," Selby thought and his stomach rumbled like an earthquake. "He was all set to leave and now, because of the spots I painted on him, he's going to stay! If I don't get him out of here soon, I'll die!"

Suddenly another light went on in Selby's head and a smile flickered across his lips.

"That's it!" he thought. "I'll pretend I'm starving! Then they'll *have* to feed me!"

Selby staggered around in circles with his tongue out and then fell down in a faint.

"Heavens!" yelled Mrs Trifle. "Selby's collapsed! He needs food!"

"Nonsense," Thornton said, adding milk to the blender and turning it on. "He's just having a sudden snooze. Snoozes are the first steps to good health. Leave him alone and he'll come round in a while."

Selby lay on the floor for minutes, as visions of rare steaks and sausages danced in his mind. He remembered the lovely dinner the Trifles made for him last Christmas. But most of all he remembered the peanut prawns that had been thrown away.

He opened one eye and noticed that he was alone in the kitchen with Thornton. Suddenly something in Selby, snapped.

"I can't stand it a second longer!" he thought. "If that looney thinks he can do this to me, I'll lunch on his leg!"

Selby jumped to his feet and bared his teeth, lunging towards Thornton's hairy legs so quickly that the startled man slopped carrot milkshake all over his face.

"Help!" Thornton screamed. "Selby's gone mad! He's trying to bite me!"

In a flash, Dr and Mrs Trifle dashed into the kitchen only to find Selby lying on the floor, looking around with big, innocent eyes.

"He did! He tried to bite me!" Thornton screamed.

"Rubbish," Mrs Trifle said, looking at where the carrot juice had washed the blue spots off Thornton's nose. "Selby's never bitten anyone in his life. It's completely un-Selbylike. But look!" she said, handing Thornton the mirror. "Your spots are gone."

That evening, after the confused Thornton had roared off back to the city, the Trifles sat down once again to their favourite fancy food from The Spicy Onion.

"I'm sure Thornton's right about eating healthy foods," Mrs Trifle said as she looked down at a plate full of barbecued oysters in mango sauce. "But there are times when it's fun to eat things just because they taste good. Don't you agree?"

"Yes, I do," said Dr Trifle as he plunged his fork into a pickled baby bamboo shoot, making sure there was a bit of bacon rind on top.

"And so do I!" thought Selby who felt like screaming it out loud.

Fortunately he couldn't talk because his mouth was stuffed with peanut prawns.

UP THE CREEK
WITHOUT A
DOG PADDLE

It was the day of the annual Flat-Out Four-Footed Dog Race across Kookaburra Flats and all the dogs in town, including Selby, had been taken to Mount Gumboot for the start of the race.

"Race, schmace," Selby thought as he looked around him at the other dogs. "Not the sort of thing a thinking, feeling dog like myself would ever really *want* to do. I mean, all that sweat and tired muscles — and for what? Last year Constable Long's dog, Streak, won a year's supply of Dry-Mouth Dog Biscuits and the poor beggar hasn't finished them yet. Even if I *could* win the race, I wouldn't want to. Just the thought of another one of those wretched biscuits is enough to make me gag. Of course, as the mayor's dog," he added thoughtfully, "I have a certain social responsibility. I know she'd be hurt if I didn't go in the race, but at least she won't mind if I come last."

"On your marks," Mrs Trifle said, raising the starting pistol and giving Selby a pat on the head with the other hand. "Get set!"

"Last year," Selby thought, "I think I may have embarrassed her just a little by starting off at a stroll when all the other dogs got away like greyhounds. This year I'll run flat-out with the rest of them till we round that rock and then I'll break into a leisurely walk as soon as I'm out of sight and all the owners are driving back to the finish line in Bogusville."

Selby looked around and saw Streak on one side and Hamish the sheepdog on the other, both straining at their owner's leads.

"Go!" Mrs Trifle yelled, firing the pistol. And Selby and the rest of the dogs tore away in a cloud of dust.

Selby was only slightly behind the pack when they rounded the rock and he ducked back into its shadow for a rest.

"So long, mates," Selby said, leaning back on one elbow and watching as Hamish suddenly left the pack and came running back.

"What's this?" Selby thought. "The dog's lost his sense of direction."

Hamish barked excitedly at Selby and then began snapping at his heels.

"Hey!" Selby yelled, knowing that Hamish couldn't understand but not caring. "Stop that! What do you think I am, a stray sheep?"

Hamish gave him one good bite on the leg and then another.

"The dog's gone mad," Selby thought as he got up and started running after the other dogs. "He thinks I'm a blinkin' sheep! Ouch!" he screamed. "You're crazy! You've chased too many sheep, Hamish! It's gone to your head! Stop it! If you don't stop, someone's going to get — yooooooowwwwwwww! Get away from me you four-legged torture chamber!"

Just then Selby noticed a wombat hole just big enough to squeeze into, and too big for

Hamish. He tore into the hole and waited for a few minutes till Hamish had given up hope of herding Selby back to Bogusville. Finally he heard Hamish's footsteps as he ran after the other dogs.

"Now's the time," Selby said, strolling along and sniffing the odd flower, "for that pleasant walk I've been looking forward to."

And as he walked — possibly inspired by the wandering poet Whittlebone Jones — a few raindrops fell and he wrote a poem in his head:

"Oh little drops
And big ones, too,
How you like me
And I like you."

But it began to pour and when Selby reached Bogusville Creek it was a roaring river instead of the usual trickle. On the other side, most of the dogs from the race had stopped and were barking.

"Oh, no you don't," Selby thought. "Nobody's going to talk me into trying to cross that mess. I'm going to turn around and head straight back to Mount Gumboot and see if I can get a lift into town."

Just as he was about to go, Selby heard a bark from the middle of the river. There, clinging to a branch, was Hamish, and the water was rising dangerously around him.

"I can't just leave him there," Selby thought, wondering if he could, and then thinking that it wouldn't be the proper thing for the mayor's dog to do. "If I can get up this rivergum and climb out on that branch ... well, it's worth a try."

Selby took a running jump onto the low branch and made his way over the raging river to where Hamish clung just below him. He leaned down off the branch, holding on with his paws and dangling his tail towards the stranded sheepdog.

"Stay calm," Selby said, feeling anything but calm himself. "Just grab my tail and I'll pull you to safety."

With this, Hamish let out a howl and then sank his teeth into Selby's tail with all his might and didn't let go.

"Yiiiiiiiiiiiii!" Selby screamed, and he dropped from the branch into the river and was carried off with Hamish still clinging to his tail. "Let go, you maniac! Let go! Help!"

Selby and Hamish tumbled over and over in the muddy water as they tore along with the current. Selby grabbed at logs and branches, but every time he caught anything, Hamish's weight pulled him away and they tumbled back into the water and further downstream.

Finally, just when Selby thought they would surely drown, he caught a long branch and dragged himself from the water with Hamish still holding on with his teeth.

"Okay," he gasped, shaking his tail and trying to get rid of the sheepdog, "we're saved. Now let go! Let go!"

Hamish was so frightened that Selby's yelling made him panic and he bit harder.

"Stop it! Yooooooooowwwwwwww!" Selby yelled, jumping to his feet and tearing along, looking back at Hamish and not noticing that Bogusville Creek had taken them right to Bogusville and that he and Hamish were headed straight for the finish line of the Flat-Out Four-Footed Dog Race. "Yipe! Yiiii! Yooooowww!"

"And look at that!" Postie Paterson yelled, as the crowd cheered and Selby and Hamish crossed the finish line. "Selby's won the race! He wins this year's grand prize — a two-year supply of Dry-Mouth Dog Biscuits!"

"Crikey!" Selby mumbled to himself as he finally prised Hamish loose from his tail. "Why is it I only seem to win when I'm trying to lose?"

IN THE SPIRIT OF THINGS

"This house is haunted," Mrs Trifle said one evening as she and Dr Trifle sat watching a TV program called *Australian Spirits, Then and Now*, which was hosted by the famous ghost hunter, Myrene Spleen. "I keep hearing footsteps running in the hall at night and there's no one there. I'm sure it's a ghost."

"It's probably just Selby getting up to nibble a dog biscuit," Dr Trifle said.

Selby's ears shot up like rockets.

"I'm not the one making the noises," he thought. "At night I tiptoe around like a cat so I won't wake the Trifles. But of course it can't be a ghost because there aren't any such things."

"It can't be Selby," Mrs Trifle said. "He tiptoes around like a cat. No, I think it's a ghost and I'm going to ring Myrene right now and see what she can do about it."

Three days later Myrene Spleen raced down the Trifles' driveway carrying a large box that said *Ghost Hunter's Kit* on the top. "Spleen's the name and spooks are my game," she said, giving Mrs Trifle a bonecrushing handshake. "Take me to the spirit spot and I'll get to the bottom of this, quick smart."

"Whatever it is, it runs up and down the hall and makes a racket," Mrs Trifle said.

"That's spook-like behaviour all right," Myrene said, snatching a bucket from the box. "And I can feel its presence."

"You can feel a ghost?" Dr Trifle said, looking at his hands.

"I get all tingly when there's a spook around," Myrene said with a shiver. "By the way, I did some research before I came to Bogusville and it's my guess you're being haunted by none other than the ghost of Brumby Bill."

"Brumby Bill?" Dr Trifle said. "But he built the first house in Bogusville. He's been dead for years," he added, suddenly realising what he'd said.

"Precisely. He came to this area a hundred years ago with his dog to get away from the city. Gradually other people settled here and built houses," Myrene said. "You don't have to tell me about Brumby Bill, I know his story back to front."

"But why would he want to haunt us?" Mrs Trifle asked, wondering why anyone would want to know a story back to front.

"My theory is that he hates what Bogusville has become."

"But Bogusville hasn't become anything," Mrs Trifle said. "It's just another country town."

"It was peaceful bush when Brumby Bill lived here and now he thinks it's ruined. And who better to haunt than you, the mayor," Myrene said, pouring a tin of white paint in the bucket. "He thinks that if he can scare *you* away then the whole town will pack up and go. Would you like him exorcised?"

"Heavens no. He gets quite enough exercise dashing up and down the hall."

"Not *exercise, exorcise*. Exorcism is just a fancy word for getting rid of a spirit. How about it?"

"Well, yes, I suppose so," Mrs Trifle said, wondering why ghost hunters didn't use simple words like everyone else.

"Won't you need television cameras and electronic ghost sensors and super-sensitive, quadro-gyric, scintillating, movement-activated microphones?" asked Dr Trifle who liked fancy words as much as anyone.

"The best way to catch a spook is to splash him with a bucket of paint," Myrene said. "It's an old-fashioned method but it usually works."

"Won't the paint go right through him?" Mrs Trifle asked, wondering how she would ever clean the paint out of her carpets.

"Not if it catches him when he's not looking. I'll wait till I feel his presence with my psychic powers and then pull the rope that tips the bucket. *Glop, slop* — down comes the paint. Then I'll snap the photo. Ghosts don't like to be photographed. He won't be back after that. And don't worry about your carpets," Myrene added. "This paint washes off in water."

"I guess it's worth a try," Mrs Trifle said. "Anything to get a good night's sleep."

"That's the spirit!" Myrene said, giggling after she said it. "Now lock that dog out so he won't get in the way. And you and Dr Trifle can go to bed. I'll do the rest."

"Ghosts, schmosts," Selby said as he lay under a bush in the front garden. "Locked out of my own house just because of a silly ghost hunt. If I don't freeze out here, I'll starve. I'm so hungry I could even eat a Dry-Mouth Dog Biscuit!"

Selby climbed up the jacaranda next to the side window and peered in at the ghost hunter who sat in the hall with her camera in one hand and the rope in the other.

"Psychic powers, piffle!" Selby thought. "The woman's sound asleep and she thinks she's going to catch a ghost. What rubbish! Whether or not she knows it," Selby added, "the Trifles left this window unlocked and Myrene's about to have a visitor."

Selby eased himself onto the window ledge and then slowly raised the window. He leaned in and put a leg in front of Myrene's face, waving his paw in front of her.

"A ghost could be doing a tapdance in front of her and she'd sleep through it," he thought. "That does it, I'm going in for a bite to eat, ghost hunt or no ghost hunt."

Selby crept down the hall to the kitchen and quietly crunched a couple of dog biscuits.

"If only I could just stay inside for the night," he thought. "Only then the Trifles would figure out that I opened an unlocked window and climbed in. They'd know they weren't dealing with an ordinary dog and it would be just a matter of time till my (*gulp*) secret would be out. Oh, well, out in the cold I go."

Selby was heading back down the hall when the sleeping Myrene Spleen suddenly jumped to her feet and yelled, "I've got the feeling! I've got the feeling! He's here!" And with this she pulled the rope.

"Help!" Selby screamed as the paint hit him with a glop and a slop and Myrene's camera flashed at the same time. "Get me out of here!"

He tore down the hall, hurled himself through the air — narrowly missing the screaming woman — and dived out the open window.

"I'm finished!" he said, hosing off the paint with the garden sprinkler. "It's over. As soon as they look at that photo they'll know that I climbed a tree and broke in through the hall window. I'm done. I'd better go and confess right now."

Selby slunk towards the front door just as Myrene burst out on the way to her car.

"Look at the dog!" she screamed, waving a photograph at Dr and Mrs Trifle. "I was wrong. It wasn't the ghost of Brumby Bill. It was the ghost of Brumby Bill's dog!"

Selby stared at the picture of himself, covered in paint, leaping through the air towards the window.

"It's the first dog ghost that's ever been photographed! And a talking dog ghost, too! Did you hear him say, 'Get me out of here!?' He won't be back to haunt you. This is great! It'll be my best TV show yet!"

"That was a close call," Selby thought as he lay on the hall carpet a little later with his eyes closed, ready for sleep. "I can't wait to see Myrene Spleen on TV talking about the dog ghost and holding up that picture of me covered in paint. Well, at least I can sleep in the house again (*yawn*) now that this ghost nonsense is over."

Selby listened as the footsteps walked along the hall, passing so close to his head that he felt a slight breeze from the moving legs.

"That'll be Dr Trifle (*yawn*) heading for the kitchen to get a drink of water," he thought. "He often does that in the middle of the night."

Had Selby lifted his head at that moment and opened his eyes to look down the darkened hall, searching for the shape of Dr Trifle hurrying along in his dressing-gown; had he just lifted one eyelid a crack, as he did when he didn't want anyone to know he was peeking, instead of falling into a deep sleep, he'd have seen *that there was no one there.*

A TIP FOR SELBY

There were times when being the only talking, reading and writing dog in Australia — and as far as he knew, in the whole world — and trying to keep it a secret, was not easy. But it was a secret that Selby was determined to keep even if it killed him. On October 3rd it nearly did ...

October 3rd was clean-up day in Bogusville and Dr and Mrs Trifle had put out some old, broken furniture to be taken to the tip. It was hot and Selby was walking towards the shade of a big tree when he looked in the open drawer of an old cupboard. There, on the bottom of the drawer, was a page from a copy of the *Bogusville Banner* with his favourite comic strip, *Wonderful Wanda, Maker of Music*. Selby put his head in the drawer to read it and then he climbed right in to get out of the sun.

Wonderful Wanda was about a woman who travelled back and forth through time trying to catch the villain who had stolen her grand piano when she was a girl. The villain, Larry Low-Note, had been frightened by a trombone when he was a baby and ever since he'd hated music. He promised to put a stop to all music; not only in the present but in the past and the future as well.

"I will destroy all musical instruments," Larry Low-Note yelled as he twirled his fingers around his black moustache and stomped a violin to matchsticks. "That will put an end to all this musical nonsense forever! Ha ha ha! He he he!"

"I must stop that villain," Wanda said, tearing through time in a spaceship that looked like a kettledrum. "If there is no music there will be no joy. The hearts of people will shrivel like flowers that fall in the desert."

And whenever she said this, in every comic strip, Selby felt a tear come into his eye and his nose begin to run.

"Don't worry, Wanda," Selby said. "You'll fix that scoundrel."

And in every episode Wanda caught up to Larry Low-Note and kept him from destroying another musical instrument. But in every episode Larry tricked her and she was captured and left to die a terrible death. In the beginning of the next episode Wanda always escaped and went on with the chase.

Selby read the comic strip in the cupboard. In the end, Larry Low-Note captured her when she fell through some branches on the ground and was trapped in an orchestra pit. He tied her up and gave her to a tribe of cannibals who put her in a pot.

"It's all right, Wanda," Selby said, knowing that she'd pull out the magic conductor's baton she kept in her boot and get free. "You'll get away. I know, I've read the next episode."

Just then the cupboard tipped backward and the drawer slammed shut. Selby felt himself being lifted up onto the council truck and then bouncing along towards the Bogusville tip.

"Crumbs," Selby said, pushing on the drawer but not being able to open it because the cupboard was lying on its front. "Trapped like a rat. Let's not panic now. Hmmmmmmmmm ... I wonder how Wanda would get out of this one? I remember the time she was trapped in a pit of cobras and she played her flute to keep them from biting her. No, that won't do me much good. First of all I don't have a flute. Secondly, there aren't any cobras around. Let's see now ... Then there was the time she was tied to the railway tracks and she made a loud whistle with a blade of grass. The engine driver thought there was another train coming so he stopped the train just in time. No," he said calmly, "that's not much good to me either. Hmmmmmmmmm. I'm not going to panic. There must be a way."

Selby felt the truck stop.

"And then there was the time..." Selby thought as he suddenly remembered that the Bogusville tip was at the bottom of a cliff and that the truck would soon dump everything over the edge, including the cupboard.

"But what am I talking about!" he screamed. "Wonderful Wanda is just someone in a comic strip! I'm a real, live, thinking and feeling dog and I'm about to be dumped over a cliff! It's time to panic! Help! I don't want to die! Save me!"

Selby heard the driver get out of the truck and walk around to the back.

"What's going on here?" the driver said to a metal filing cabinet. "Who's yelling for help?"

"I am," Selby said, knowing he was giving away his secret and that he would probably be the Trifles' servant for life but not caring because it was better to be a live servant than a dead dog with a secret.

"The filing cabinet or the shopping trolley?" the puzzled driver asked.

"Neither," Selby said. "The cupboard."

"Now wait just a minute," the driver said. "Cupboards can't talk."

"Neither can filing cabinets and shopping trolleys, you nit," Selby said. "But this one has a dog in it so open the drawer and let me out before I suffocate."

The driver turned the cupboard over and very carefully opened the drawer.

"Crikey!" he said, grabbing Selby by the collar. "You really are a talking dog! I wouldn't have believed it if I hadn't heard it with my own ears. I'll be rich! Say something, dog."

"Bow wow wow," Selby said, trying to keep his secret now that he wasn't about to be dumped over the cliff.

"Don't give me that bow wow wow rubbish," the driver said, giving Selby a good shake. "Give me some proper English. You can speak it and I know you can so don't try to kid me."

"Let go of me, you drongo!" Selby said, pulling loose and jumping down from the truck. "You'll never catch me now! And don't bother telling anyone you've seen a talking dog because nobody's going to believe you."

Just then the truck started to roll and the driver found that his belt buckle was caught in the back. To make matters worse, it was headed straight for the cliff.

"Help!" the driver screamed, trying to pull his buckle loose as he tiptoed madly after the truck. "Help! Please don't let me go over the cliff!"

Selby thought for a second and then ran after the runaway truck and jumped into the cabin. He started pulling knobs and levers but the truck hurtled on towards the cliff, going faster and faster.

Suddenly he remembered a TV show he'd seen called *All About Cars*, and he jumped down to the floor and pulled up the handbrake. The truck screeched to a stop only a centimetre from the edge of the cliff.

"Sheeeesh!" Selby said, hopping out and running for home, leaving the driver to

untangle his belt buckle. "That was too close for comfort."

That evening, Mrs Trifle came home very tired.

"I need a holiday," she told Dr Trifle while Selby lay on the latest copy of the *Bogusville Banner* secretly reading *Wonderful Wanda, Maker of Music*. "I must be working too hard. Today one of the council truck drivers said he saw a talking dog so I gave him a month off work, poor man. If I don't take some time off soon," she said, looking over at Selby, "I'll be seeing talking dogs too."

"Little does she know," Selby thought and he squinted his eyes so she couldn't see them moving as he finished reading *Wonderful Wanda*, "that she's looking at one."

SELBY GAGGED

The good news was that Gary Gaggs, the corniest comedian in Australia, was back in Bogusville to do his comedy act at the Bogusville School of Arts Banquet. The bad news was that he was staying with Dr and Mrs Trifle.

"Oh, woe woe woe," Selby thought as Dr Trifle greeted his old friend at the door. "Of all the places to stay in Bogusville, why, oh why, oh why, does he have to stay here?"

"You're looking great, Blinky!" Gary said, using Dr Trifle's old nickname and shaking his hand furiously. "As for me, I just flew in from Perth and my arms are tired! Woo woo woo!"

Every time Gary told a joke he strutted around like a rooster, pumping his elbows up and down and saying, "Woo woo woo!"

"His jokes are absolutely awful!" Selby thought. "But the problem is — it's all I can do to keep from laughing at them. And if I ever laughed — if I ever even *smiled* — my secret would be out! I've got to get out of here quick!"

Selby dashed for the door but Gary reached out and grabbed him by the collar.

"Selby's a real locksmith dog," Gary said, patting him on the head.

"A locksmith dog?" Dr Trifle asked.

"Yes. He just made a *bolt* for the door! Woo woo woo!" Gary boomed. "Seriously though, I had a kelpie once and I put him in some sheepdog trials."

"Is that so?" Dr Trifle said. "How'd he do?"

"He was found *not guilty*! Woo woo woo!" Gary laughed. "But seriously, I was going to sell him but he got his tail caught in a gate. I had to sell him *wholesale* because I couldn't *retail* him! Woo woo woo!"

"Oh, that's very funny," Dr Trifle said instead of laughing. "But you never really had a dog, did you Gary?"

"I had a dog just like your Selby but he got lost."

"Isn't that sad. What did you do?"

"Nothing. I was going to put an ad in the newspaper but I knew it wouldn't do any good."

"Why not?"

"Because he couldn't read! Woo woo woo!" Gary screeched, pumping his arms up and down, giving Selby time to dart out the door and into the bushes before he laughed. "Hey! Why don't you bring Selby to the banquet tonight and I can tell some more dog gags?"

That night the Trifles sat at the end of a long table next to Gary Gaggs. Selby was on Mrs Trifle's lap watching as the comedian ate masses of food, lots of it falling on his checked shirt.

Finally, just as the Peach Piffle dessert arrived, Gary Gaggs stood up.

"Thank you very much for inviting me here tonight," he started. "It's too bad I'm on a diet. By the way, did you hear about the cannibal who went on a diet? He only ate pygmies. Woo woo woo!"

"Oh, wow! That's a good one," Selby thought as he fought back a smile and the guests roared with laughter. "He only ate pygmies!"

"But seriously, folks. This food reminds me of my mother-in-law's cooking. My mother-in-law is a beautiful lady. She's sixty years old and still has skin like a peach. But did you ever see the skin of a sixty-year-old peach?! Woo woo woo!"

"A sixty-year-old peach!" Selby squealed as he gasped for breath. "I love his mother-in-law jokes!"

"But seriously, she's a lovely lady. I call her *my fare lady*. She used to be a bus conductor. Woo woo woo!"

"Oh, I get it!" Selby thought putting a paw over his mouth. "My *fare* lady! That's great!"

"She's lovely," Gary went on. "She only has one false tooth. You'd never know it was false if it didn't come out in conversation. Woo woo woo!"

Selby put his head under the tablecloth and let out a giggle while everyone howled with laughter.

"But seriously now, folks," Gary continued. "My mother-in-law used to run a pet shop. One day I went there to buy a pet. She said, 'I've got a cockatoo that lays square eggs and talks.' I said, 'A cockatoo that lays square eggs and talks? What does it say?' And she said, '*Ouch!*' Woo woo woo!"

Selby squealed with laughter.

"I can't stand it," he thought. "I've got to get out of here before anyone realises I'm laughing."

"So I said to her, I said," Gary went on, "'I don't want a bird, I want a dog.' And she put a dog up on the counter. Now wait a minute. Where's that dog? Get up here, Selby."

"Gulp," Selby thought. "What does he want me for?"

Selby spied an open door and was about to run for it when Gary grabbed him and put him on the table.

"She said, 'This dog is pure Irish Setter.' I said, 'Oh really?' and she said, 'No, O'Reilly.' Woo woo woo!"

"O'Reilly! That's great!" Selby thought, feeling everyone's eyes looking at him. "But if I can't keep a straight face I'm a done dog. If only his jokes weren't so funny."

"So I said to my mother-in-law, I said, 'This dog has no nose. How does he smell?' And she said, 'Terrible!' Woo woo woo!"

Selby put a paw over his mouth to hide a creeping smile as Gary gripped his collar with one hand and patted him with the other.

"But seriously folks," Gary continued. "She told me that the dog was a real watchdog. And she was right. I took him home to guard my house and he sat down and watched TV. Woo woo woo!"

"I can't stand it any longer," Selby said, choking and sputtering and burying his face in a serviette to keep from laughing — all of which only made the people laugh more.

"But he *was* a watchdog," Gary continued. "That night when I was out the house was robbed. The dog watched the whole thing! Woo woo woo! But seriously, the dog is a police dog and he's going to investigate the crime. He isn't sure who did it but he has … Come on, folks, he has … what? I'm tired of doing all the talking. You tell me."

"I know, I know!" Selby thought as sweat streamed down his face. "I know the punchline and if anyone tells it, I'm a goner. There's no way I can keep from laughing. Save me!"

With this, Selby started running but, with Gary still holding his collar, what happened was that the tablecloth and sixty-two bowls of Peach Piffle came tearing towards him, hitting Gary Gaggs who let go of Selby and fell to the floor covered in dessert. There was silence for a moment and then everyone, including Gary, roared with laughter as Selby ran the length of the bare table, past the howling guests, and out the door. He didn't stop running till he collapsed in a fit of laughter in the middle of Bogusville Reserve.

"The dog isn't sure who did it," Selby screeched as he rolled on the ground and licked off a chunk of Peach Piffle, "but he has a good *lead*! Woo woo woo! That man is the funniest comedian in the whole world!"

SOMETHING FISHY AT BUNYA-BUNYA CRESCENT

Dr and Mrs Trifles' old friend Dr Septimus C. Squirt was due at the Trifles' house at any minute from the Great Barrier Reef to talk to the Bogusville branch of The Friends of Furry Animals, recently renamed The Friends of Furry and *Fishy* Animals, about his study of dolphin language.

"Dolphin language," Selby thought as he went into the kitchen and looked at the polished pewter trophy cup with a ribbon around it that was to be Dr Squirt's gift for giving the lecture. "He's been listening to the squeaks and bleeps of dolphins and the songs of humpback whales for ten years and I'll bet he still doesn't have a clue what they're talking about."

Then, as Selby turned to go back to the lounge room where the guests were waiting, he knocked the polished pewter trophy cup on the floor with his tail, breaking it neatly in two.

"Crumbs!" he said, dashing for a tube of Cosmic-Clutch Multi-Use Glue. "I've got to glue it back together quickly! I wonder if this is any good for mending broken polished pewter trophy cups," he thought as he read the label. "Hmmmmm. Let's see now. It says, *Especially good for mending broken polished pewter trophy cups*," he said forgetting to read the bit that said:

WARNING!

AVOID GETTING THIS GLUE ON YOU IF YOU KNOW WHAT'S GOOD FOR YOU! IGNORE THIS WARNING AND YOU'LL BE SORRY.

"I only hope it hardens quickly," Selby said, as he smeared the Cosmic-Clutch Multi-Use Glue on the broken edges of the cup with his paws and then tied it together with the ribbon.

Just then Dr Squirt arrived at the front door holding a life-sized plastic replica of a dolphin.

"I'm sorry I'm late, Blinky," he said, using Dr Trifle's old nickname. "Boy, am I thirsty! It's been a long hot drive. I'll get a drink of water from the kitchen if you don't mind."

"By all means," Dr Trifle said as his old friend put the dolphin on the floor and dashed for the kitchen. "It's right through those —" he started, but by then Dr Squirt was through them.

"Now, where's a glass?" Dr Squirt asked, glancing idly at Selby and not knowing that he was glancing idly at the only dog in Australia who could have answered his question. "Ahah!" Dr Squirt said, spying the polished pewter trophy cup and filling it with water. "This will have to do."

Dr Squirt then put the cup down beside the sink and dashed back to the lounge room, not knowing that he'd drunk out of his gift.

"Thank goodness it didn't fall apart," Selby thought as he followed Dr Squirt and lay down on the floor next to the life-sized plastic replica of a dolphin, grabbing it in his front paws as he waited for Dr Squirt's talk to begin.

Dr Squirt looked around at The Friends of Furry and Fishy Animals and tried to speak but found to his horror that he couldn't get his mouth open.

"Mmmmmmmmm," he said, waving his arms at his audience and trying to tell them that his teeth and lips were stuck together (but not knowing that a bit of Cosmic-Clutch Multi-Use Glue from the drinking water had got into his mouth). "Huuuuuuuuuuuuuuuuuuuuuuuuuuuuu mmmmmmmmmmmmmmmmmmmmmmmmmmmm nnnnnnnnnnnnnnnnnnnnnnnnn!"

A murmur went around the room and then silence fell as Dr Squirt made a series of non-human sounds like, "*gleep gleep squeak bleek*" and just plain, "*bleeeeeeeeeeeeeeeeeeeeeeeeeeeeeeeeep!*" as he pulled at his lips with his hands.

"I do believe that Septimus has finally cracked the code," Dr Trifle said at last. "He's speaking to us in perfect dolphin!"

"Brilliant!" someone screamed and deafening applause broke out with shouts of "*Bravo!*", "*Magnifico!*" and "*Good on ya!*"

"Good grief! He's got glue in his gob!" Selby thought as he watched Dr Squirt screech again and again with his mouth closed. "If someone doesn't do something fast his gob-opening days will be over!"

Dr Squirt fell squirming to the floor still squeaking and bleeping.

"Now he's imitating the way a dolphin swims!" Mrs Trifle said. "It must all be part of the way they communicate. I think he wants us to figure out what he's saying!"

"This is awful!" Selby thought. "He's glued for good! And it's all my fault for breaking the polished pewter trophy cup! How embarrassing!"

With this Selby jumped to his feet to go and be embarrassed somewhere else when he noticed that the life-sized plastic dolphin replica jumped up with him.

"Crikey!" he thought, suddenly realising that his paws were stuck to the dolphin's tail. "It's got me! If I don't pull it loose quickly, I'll have to follow it around for the rest of my life!"

Selby pushed it away with his paws frantically and then pounded it against the floor, but it was still no looser than when he started. In a panic he started spinning around and around in the middle of the room like an Olympic discus thrower about to throw a discus — or a dolphin.

"What's happening to Selby?" Mrs Trifle screamed, and everyone except the squeaking and bleeping Dr Squirt gathered around as Selby spun faster and faster, making a whooshing noise like a huge fan.

Then, with a great *pop* like the one you can make by putting your finger in your mouth — only louder — the dolphin broke loose and shot through the air hitting Dr Squirt in the mouth, making another loud *pop*.

The Friends of Furry and Fishy Animals watched as Dr Squirt flexed his jaw back and forth and stuck his tongue out a few times, just to make sure it was still there.

"That was the oddest thing," Dr Squirt said. "My mouth was stuck shut and I couldn't for the life of me get it open. But thanks to your dog and my dolphin, I think I'll be okay now."

"It seems like the dolphin taught *you* to talk this time," Dr Trifle said with a laugh. "But I still don't know what happened. Why was Selby spinning around like that? He hates any kind of exercise."

"If only he could talk," Mrs Trifle said with a sigh, "I'm sure he could tell us a thing or two."

"Or maybe even three," Selby thought as he headed out the door for a walk rather than listen to a boring lecture. "But let's just say that my lips are sealed — just as Dr Squirt's were."

FOOL OF FORTUNE

"That lovely gypsy fortune-teller down at the Bogusville Fair, Madame Mascara, read my palm today. She said that I'd have a long and happy life and that we needn't worry about getting old because our children will look after us," Mrs Trifle told Dr Trifle as she quickly made three peanut butter and banana sandwiches.

"It sounds like the kind of thing fortune-tellers tell everyone," Dr Trifle said politely. "I wouldn't take it seriously, especially as we don't have any children."

"Maybe she means Selby. He's like a child to us," Mrs Trifle said, handing Dr Trifle a sandwich. "Here's your bananabutter sandwich."

"Thank you," Dr Trifle said, taking the sandwich and looking at Selby who lay at his feet pretending not to listen. Dr Trifle wondered how Selby could possibly look after them when they were old. "By the way, who's the extra bananabutter sandwich for?"

"It's for Madame Mascara," Mrs Trifle said. "She said she'd never heard of a bananabutter sandwich so I promised to bring her one. She said she'd tell Selby's fortune for free if I did. Wasn't that kind of her?"

"Fortune, schmortune," Selby thought as he opened his eyes a crack and peeked at the Trifles. "It's all superstition. I don't believe a word of it. Nobody can see into the future."

"What if … ?" Dr Trifle began, pausing for a minute to scrape some peanut butter off the roof of his mouth only to get it stuck on his finger. "What if Madame Thing-am-e sees something terrible in Selby's future? You know, something really awful."

"You mean like he's going to snuff it tomorrow?" Mrs Trifle asked.

"I beg your pardon?" Dr Trifle said, licking the glob of peanut butter off his finger only to get it stuck on the roof of his mouth again.

"You know, peg it. Turn up his toes. In a word: *die*," Mrs Trifle explained.

"You certainly do have a way with words," Dr Trifle said. "But yes, that's what I meant."

"When fortune-tellers see something dreadful in someone's future, they never tell it. They keep it to themselves," Mrs Trifle said. "They don't want their customers wandering around all worried just because they only have one more day to live. That wouldn't be very much fun, would it?"

"No, I suppose not," Dr Trifle said, scraping the peanut butter onto his finger again.

"Ooops!" Mrs Trifle said suddenly. "I'd better get Selby down to the fairgrounds before Madame Mascara packs her tent and goes away."

"Me — Selby — snuff it tomorrow? Such rubbish! If it was going to happen," Selby thought as Mrs Trifle led him towards the gypsy's tent, "I'm sure Madame Mascara would be the last to know. I laugh at fortune-tellers. Ha ha and double ho ho! It's all bunk."

"Oh, how exciting!" Madame Mascara said, reaching out a ring-covered hand and grabbing the peanut butter and banana sandwich and biting a chunk out of it. "A bananabutter sandwich. It must be very healthy."

"I'm sure it is," Mrs Trifle said, lifting Selby onto the chair next to the fortune-teller.

"Now, let's see what the future holds for your little dog. Hmmmmmmmm," Madame Mascara said, puzzling over the cracks and lines on Selby's paw. "Dog feet aren't quite like

people feet, are they? I'd better gaze into my crystal ball instead."

Selby watched as Madame Mascara waved her hand back and forth in front of the crystal ball like a window-washer in a hurry. Inside the glass he saw her reflection: an upside down Madame Mascara waving back.

Suddenly a strange look came over the fortune-teller's face. "Oh, no!" she screamed and accidentally knocked the crystal ball off the table and onto Selby's foot. There was a *gurgle gurgle* sound from her throat and then a *burble burble* and she fell to the ground in a faint.

"Madame Mascara! Madame Mascara!" Mrs Trifle yelled as she fanned the woman's face with a pack of fortune-telling cards. "Are you all right?"

Selby watched as the fortune-teller's eyes flickered open and she raised her head.

"I'm okay, Mrs Trifle," she said finally. "It's just that I saw something dreadful in the crystal ball. I'm afraid I can't say anything. It wouldn't be polite."

Selby stood stock-still for a second, sweating like a sprinter.

"Oh, no! It can't be!" he thought suddenly as he tore from the tent. "She's seen something terrible about me and she won't say anything. The jig is up! It's curtains! I've had it! I'm history! I'm going to snuff it tomorrow and she's worried about being polite! Oh, woe woe woe."

Selby ran across the fields picking four-leaf clovers and touching wood as he went and keeping an eye out for black cats that might cross his path and ladders that he might accidentally go under and mirrors that might break.

"Why am I worrying about broken mirrors? They give you seven years' bad luck. I'd give anything right now for seven years' bad luck!" Selby said as he climbed under the fence at The Friendly Duffer Riding Stables and searched the rubbish barrels for worn-out horseshoes that might give him good luck. "I was a happy dog till I met that ring-covered crystal-gazing soothsayer."

When Selby finally came home that evening, dragging a bag full of good luck charms which he hid in the garage, he slipped into the lounge room where Dr Trifle was reading a book called *The Beginner's Book of Future Predicting*.

"I might as well talk to the Trifles," he thought. "It's going to be all over for me (*sniff*) tomorrow. I might as well tell Dr Trifle that I can speak. I so want to thank him and Mrs Trifle for being so good to me (*sniff*) all these years."

Selby put his paws up on the doctor's knee and cleared his throat, ready to speak. Dr Trifle lowered his book and looked at Selby.

"Had a hard day have you, old pooch?" Dr Trifle said, suddenly finding a bit of peanut butter still stuck to the roof of his mouth and trying to get it loose with his tongue. "Hish snot eashy been a yog, ish it? I mean," he said, and then he gave up with his tongue and scraped the peanut butter off on his finger, "it's not easy being a dog, is it?"

"Not when you're about to snuff it tomorrow," Selby thought.

Just then Mrs Trifle burst into the room.

"Oh, there's Selby! Thank goodness he's okay," she said, stroking Selby's ears. "He got a terrible fright at the fair. Madame Mascara fainted and knocked her crystal ball on his foot, poor baby. It must have hurt him terribly. He went running off and I never thought I'd see him again."

"What happened to her?" Dr Trifle asked.

"She was too polite to say anything at first and pretended she'd been upset by something she saw in the crystal ball, but it seems she's allergic to peanut butter. She didn't know that bananabutter sandwiches have peanut butter in them. One chomp and she dropped like a rock. We can thank our lucky stars that she was okay again in a minute."

"And what did she say about Selby's future?" Dr Trifle asked.

"She says he'll live a long and happy life and that his children will look after him when he's old," Mrs Trifle said.

"But he doesn't have any children," Dr Trifle said, licking the peanut butter glob from his finger and swallowing it.

"She probably means us, dear. I've always thought he looked on us as his human children. Oh, if only Selby could talk I'm sure he'd have some tales to tell," Mrs Trifle said and she saw a faint doggy smile spread across Selby's lips.

SELBY CRACKS
A CASE

"The portrait of me is missing from the council chambers!" Mrs Trifle exclaimed to Sergeant Short and Constable Long as she burst into the police station with Selby at her side. "I just came back from a weekend away and ... and ... and it's gone!"

"Your portrait?" Sergeant Short said, jumping to his feet. "Is that the one your husband painted, the one of you with your eyes crossed?"

"Yes. I know it's not a great painting," Mrs Trifle said, "but Dr Trifle painted it for me as a gift so it means a lot to me."

"There's no need to panic, Mrs Mayor," said Sergeant Short, who had just watched the latest episode of *Inspector Quigley's Casebook* on TV about a butler who stole a valuable painting. "I'll have the culprit behind bars before long or my name's not Short."

"And I'll help," Constable Long, who loved solving mysteries, said, "or my name's not Long."

"Do whatever you can," Mrs Trifle, who had just watched the same episode of *Inspector Quigley's Casebook*, said as Selby thought for a moment about long and short names. "But whatever we do we have to keep the theft a secret from Dr Trifle. If he knows that someone's stolen his painting he'll be most upset."

"Don't worry, Mrs Mayor," Sergeant Short assured her. "We're almost as good at keeping secrets as we are at solving mysteries."

That evening, Sergeant Short rang Mrs Trifle at her home.

"I have rounded up three suspects," he whispered into the telephone, "and I've asked them to come to the scene of the crime, the council chambers, tonight, so that I can expose the culprit. Can you come too?"

"Why, yes," Mrs Trifle whispered back, remembering that Inspector Quigley liked to gather all the suspects together at the scene of the crime when he exposed a culprit. "Dr Trifle is working away quietly in his workshop. I'll just pretend that I'm taking my dog Selby for a walk. He'll never know I'm at the council chambers."

When Mrs Trifle and Selby arrived at the scene of the crime Sergeant Short was pacing up and down in front of the suspects — Postie Paterson, Melanie Mildew and Phil Philpot — smoking a pipe and wearing a quilted dressing-gown just like Inspector Quigley.

"But just a minute, Sergeant," Mrs Trifle said, "there must be some mistake. I'm sure none of these good people has done anything wrong."

"In the business of criminal investigation," Sergeant Short said, quoting Inspector Quigley, "you can never be sure of anything. Often it's the least likely people who turn to a life of crime."

"Oh boy, this is exciting!" Selby thought, suddenly wondering if all three suspects were international portrait thieves.

"After careful investigation I've established that the painting was removed yesterday at exactly midday while you were out of town," Sergeant Short said, blowing a puff of smoke in the air, "by a man wearing an overcoat with the collar turned up, a hat pulled down over his eyes and a false moustache."

"What a great piece of detective work!" Selby, who had also watched the latest episode of *Inspector Quigley's Casebook*, thought. "I wonder how he worked it out."

"How did you work that out?" Mrs Trifle, who was also curious, asked.

"I worked it out from information supplied to me by Constable Long," he said, pointing his pipe stem at Constable Long. "After some discussion he revealed to me a bit of information that cracked the case, a vital clue."

"Cracked the case! A vital clue!" Selby thought. "This is great! Inspector Quigley is always cracking cases and finding vital clues."

"And what clue was that?" Mrs Trifle asked.

"Constable Long informed me that he had seen a man wearing an overcoat with the collar turned up, a hat pulled down over his eyes and a false moustache sneaking suspiciously out of the council chambers with the painting in question under his arm. Unfortunately he didn't think anything of it at the time. Now!" Sergeant Short said, suddenly doing a Quigley-like spin and pointing his pipe at his first suspect. "Postie Paterson, where were you at the time of the crime?"

"At the time of the crime," Postie said, trying not to giggle. "That's a good rhyme."

"Please be serious and answer the question, Postie," Sergeant Short said sharply.

"Sorry, Sergeant. At the time of the crime I was in the post office sorting mail," Postie said. "I can prove it. About twenty people came in to buy stamps at midday. They'll all be witnesses that I was there and not out stealing paintings."

"Ahah! But is it not true that you once lived in the city and that you were a *butler*?" asked Sergeant Short, who knew from *Inspector Quigley's Casebook* that butlers were the ones who usually did it.

"No! No! No!" yelled Postie, who was also an Inspector Quigley fan. "You can't pin that rap on me! I'm innocent! I was never a butler."

"This is getting more exciting than TV!" Selby thought, wondering where the questioning was leading.

"And you?" Sergeant Short said, turning to his second suspect, Melanie Mildew. "Were you ever a butler?"

"I was a maid once," Melanie said with a yawn.

"That's not good enough!" Sergeant Short said, coughing on some smoke and spinning around to his third suspect. "How about you, Phil Philpot? Were you ever a butler?"

"No. I was a *bugler* in the army," said Phil, "but I was never a butler. If you change the *g* in bugler for a *t* then you have *butler*."

"Then you expect me to believe that you didn't steal the portrait of the cross-eyed mayor — I mean the cross-eyed portrait of the mayor?" Sergeant Short said, wagging his finger in Phil Philpot's face the way Inspector Quigley always did when he was trying to get his suspects to blush and give themselves away.

"I can prove I was in my restaurant, The Spicy Onion, at the time of the crime," Phil said, blushing, as he always did when people

151

wagged fingers in his face. "I have thirty witnesses — they were all having lunch in my restaurant at the time. They'll tell you I was peeling carrots at exactly midday and not stealing paintings."

"I'm not sure this questioning is getting us anywhere," Selby thought.

Just then Selby noticed a mysterious figure wearing an overcoat with a turned-up collar, a hat pulled down over his eyes and a fake moustache, slip into the back of the chambers and hang the stolen painting on the wall.

"Crikey, it's him! It's the butler, returning the painting!" Selby thought. "Everyone's too busy trying to crack the crime. If they'd only turn around, they'd see him!"

Selby watched as the shadowy figure tiptoed towards the door.

"What can I do to get their attention?"

Selby thought. "I could scream out, '*It's him! It's the thief!*' but I'd give away my secret. Besides, they'd probably all stare at me and he'd get away. I've got to do something!"

Selby gave a growl and then a lot of barks as he tore past Sergeant Short, spinning him around and knocking his pipe out of his hand. The thief broke into a run but Selby jumped into the air and grabbed him by the coat.

"The thief!" Constable Long exclaimed as he grabbed the thief and knocked him to the floor. "I've got him! Help me get his disguise off."

Sergeant Short, the three suspects and Mrs Trifle gathered around the fallen man and the sergeant pulled off his hat and his false moustache.

"Dr Trifle!" Sergeant Short exclaimed. "So you're the butler — I mean, the culprit!"

"I — I — I —" Dr Trifle said, not knowing quite what to say.

"Darling, why did you do it?" Mrs Trifle cried. "Why did you turn to a life of crime? And why did you steal your own painting?"

"Please forgive me, I didn't steal it," Dr Trifle said, getting to his feet and dusting himself off. "I only borrowed it back to uncross your eyes. I wanted to do it while you were out of town to surprise you, but it took till today to get it right. See?" he said, pointing to the portrait.

"He's right," Selby thought as he looked up at the repainted portrait, "the eyes aren't crossed

any more. In fact they're *very* uncrossed —
they're looking off in different directions."

"Oh, darling," Mrs Trifle said, giving
Dr Trifle a mayorly hug, "it's a wonderful
surprise. Of course you're forgiven."

"And so ends another day and another
mystery," Selby said, quoting what Inspector
Quigley always said at the end of his program,
and he dashed home to watch the latest episode
of *Inspector Quigley's Casebook*, *The Case of the
Quick-Thinking Dog*.

BACKWORD

Well there you have it. Lots of exciting narrow escapes but my secret is still a secret. And it's going to stay, that way forever! Touch wood. (I'm touching wood because I'm lying on the bare floor under the dining table.) Anyway, the Trifles are still asleep so it's safe to keep writing.

Ooooope! I think I hear Dr. Trifle coming! Oh no! He's about to lift up the table cloth and see this note! I'll have to eat it!

Help!

Selby

P.T.O.

P.S. I had this note in my gob and was about to swallow when Mrs Trifle called to Dr. Trifle. He didn't lift the table cloth after all. Phew! Close call! I'd better go now. Catch you later.

S.

ABOUT THE AUTHOR

Duncan Ball is an Australian author and scriptwriter, best known for his popular books for children. Among his most-loved works are the Selby books of stories plus the collections *Selby's Selection*, *Selby's Joke Book* and *Selby's Side-splitting Joke Book*. Some of these books have also been published in New Zealand, Germany, Japan and the USA, and have won countless awards, most of which were voted by the children themselves.

Among Duncan's other books are the Emily Eyefinger series about the adventures of a girl who was born with an eye on the end of her finger, and the comedy novels *Piggott Place* and

Piggotts in Peril, about the frustrations of twelve-year-old Bert Piggott forever struggling to get his family of ratbags and dreamers out of the trouble they are constantly getting themselves into.

Duncan lives in Sydney with his wife, Jill, and their cat, Jasper. Jasper often keeps Duncan company while he's writing and has been known to help by walking on the keyboard. Once, returning to his work, Duncan found the following word had mysteriously appeared on screen: lkantawq ....

For more information about Duncan and his books, see Selby's web site at:
www.harpercollins.com.au/selby

PIGGOTT PLACE

Duncan Ball

'Tell me what I should do with my life!' Bert wailed. 'Should I catch a boat to South America? Should I learn to play the trombone? Should I start an ostrich farm? I need your help! Give me a sign, any sign!'

Sadly, Bert was talking to the only one he trusted in the whole world: Gazza, his stuffed goat. And, once again, the goat wasn't talking …

Piggott Place is a riotous but touching comedy about twelve-year-old Bert Piggott as he struggles to keep his family of dreamers, ratbags and scoundrels together. Everyone hates the Piggotts and now the council is going to evict them from their once beautiful mansion, Piggott Place. But the authorities haven't bargained on Bert and his young friend Antigone (would-be star of stage and screen) and their crazy scheme. The question is: can two kids take on a world of adults and win?

PIGGOTTS IN PERIL
Duncan Ball

Piggotts in Peril begins with the shy and sensitive Bert Piggott accidentally finding the map to pirate treasure hidden many years ago by his great-great-great-great-grandfather. At first a quest for untold wealth seems the answer to all his problems but getting it means bringing along his scheming, ratbag family. Little does he know that what lies ahead are problems that even the pessimistic Bert could never imagine: the terror of turbulent seas aboard a 'borrowed' boat, capture by pirates, being marooned on the Isle of the Dead, and more.

Piggotts in Peril is a warm, adventure-comedy about the origins of the universe, the evolution of humankind — and pirate treasure.